*W*hat the critics are saying...

ක

"Indulge yourself and enjoy the world of the sometimes dangerous but always hot, Sterling Files." ~ *The Eternal Light*

"Ms. King's stunning success with her erotic pen is much like a wizard mastering his magic always spellbinding. Yet again, Ms. King has crafted a whole new premise, which is carnally exhilarating and infectious." ~ *Love Romances*

Steele

"Sherri L. King begins her Sterling Files series with a bang." ~ *Fallen Angel Reviews*

"Ms. King has written a fascinating story with multilayered characters who will grab readers from the start. STEELE begins the Sterling Files series with a heavy duty bang and this reviewer can't wait for the next story, VICIOUS." ~ *Romance Reveiw Today*

Vicious

"This is a short but rollicking sexy story told in the spicy style, with the paranormally gifted characters Sheri King is so good at. A terrific second to an interesting contemporary paranormal suspense series." ~ *The Eternal Light*

"Sherri L. King's VICIOUS is a must read for those readers who enjoy a mixture of suspense, sex, and danger in their stories. I can't wait to read FYRE, the next book in this exciting series." ~ *Romance Reviews Today*

"Ms. King has written another action-packed, sexual fierce, no-holds-barred, paranormal book to add to her other highly acclaimed erotic series. Ms. King's characters will grab the readers by the throat, and fling them into the story, arousing their senses to a fever pitch!" ~ *Love Romances*

"I was instantly drawn into the world created by Sherri L. King in this book. I went back to Ellora's Cave and bought the first in the series fifteen pages into this book. The characters and the plot are fantastic." ~ *Fallen Angel Reviews*

Fyre

"I cannot wait to read more. I've been eating these up and reading them in one sitting." ~ *Fallen Angel Reviews*

"Engaging and provocative, Sherri L. King's FYRE will definitely heat up your night." ~ *Romance Reviews Today*

SHERRI L. KING

Sterling FILES

ELLORA'S CAVE
ROMANTICA PUBLISHING

An Ellora's Cave Romantica Publication

www.ellorascave.com

Sterling Files

ISBN 141995511X
ALL RIGHTS RESERVED.
Steele Copyright© 2005 Sherri L. King
Vicious Copyright© 2005 Sherri L. King
Fyre Copyright© 2005 Sherri L. King

Edited by Kelli Kwiatkowski.
Cover art by Darrell King.

Trade paperback Publication August 2006

Excerpt from *Manaconda* Copyright © Sherri L. King, Jaid Black, Lora Leigh 2004

Warning:

The following material contains graphic sexual content meant for mature readers. This story has been rated E–rotic by a minimum of three independent reviewers.

Ellora's Cave Publishing offers three levels of Romantica™ reading entertainment: S (S-ensuous), E (E-rotic), and X (X-treme).

S-*ensuous* love scenes are explicit and leave nothing to the imagination.

E-*rotic* love scenes are explicit, leave nothing to the imagination, and are high in volume per the overall word count. In addition, some E-rated titles might contain fantasy material that some readers find objectionable, such as bondage, submission, same sex encounters, forced seductions, and so forth. E-rated titles are the most graphic titles we carry; it is common, for instance, for an author to use words such as "fucking", "cock", "pussy", and such within their work of literature.

X-*treme* titles differ from E-rated titles only in plot premise and storyline execution. Unlike E-rated titles, stories designated with the letter X tend to contain controversial subject matter not for the faint of heart.

Also by Sherri L. King

ත

Contents

Steele

ဿ

Dedication

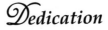

For D.

Trademarks Acknowledgement

~

The author acknowledges the trademarked status and trademark owners of the following wordmarks mentioned in this work of fiction:

Expedition: Ford Motor Company

Mini Cooper: Rover Group Limited

Prologue

ɕᴏ

"Dad, I don't want to do this."

"Well, you're going to whether you like it or not, you little bastard."

"Please don't make me, Dad, *please!* I nearly killed the last guy. I can't do this again!"

"Boy, you'll do as you're told with no more backtalk." His father reached up and cuffed him on the side of the head.

Steele looked down at the tape covering his knuckles, head ringing, and felt a sinking sensation low in his belly. Here he was, the thirteen-year-old champion of an illegal boxing ring, and all he could think about was how not to throw up.

What would the other fighter think if he knew?

Steele's father ushered him out of the small utility room that served as Steele's gym locker and dressing room. It was a strange sight, this shuffling of feet, for Steele was so much bigger than his father. He was only thirteen but he was already six feet two inches tall. And not only was he tall, he was also very well built, with bulging muscles that should have and could have graced the form of someone much older.

The boy was exceptionally good at bare-knuckles boxing, no matter his handicap of youth. His father had been taking him to these matches since he was ten years old. Steele had climbed the ladder to a certain kind of stardom among the gamblers and trainers that flocked to the illegal boxing rings. He'd never once lost a match.

But the last match had been grueling. Steele had thought, at first, that it would be his first loss in the ring, the man had been that good. But Steele's reserves of strength had not surprisingly been limitless. After thirteen rounds he'd nearly killed his opponent, so badly did he beat him.

Steele was done. He wanted no more of this world of fists and blood. He wanted out.

But how to convince his father, who was perfectly happy making money off of his boy, that it was time to quit? Steele didn't know the answer to that.

The cheers of the crowd reached his ears before he'd even made it to the ring in the center of the mass of gathered people. They had seen him coming and let out a roar of adulation as he passed through them.

Steele hated them all. It was because of them and their love of gambling that he was even here to begin with.

Steele stepped into the ring. His father eyed him stonily. "Try to make it to the tenth round before you throttle him. I've got my money on the tenth round and I sure don't want to lose it. And if you even think to end it sooner, remember my stick and stay the course. You got that boy?"

Steele nodded, putting a rubber bit in his mouth. His opponent, a large, dark-skinned man named Oscar, also stepped into the ring. The two eyed one another, each sizing the other up as they prepared themselves for the fight ahead.

The crowd roared as the two opponents stepped to the center of the ring and touched fists. Steele looked Oscar in the eyes and saw fear. It made his stomach roll sickly to know his opponent already feared him, and before the first punch was thrown no less. The bell rang and the match was started before he could even think to walk away.

Oscar immediately pummeled the thirteen-year-old with his fists, wasting no time in attacking him. But Steele barely felt the blows, his body capable of withstanding far more damage. Oscar's blows merely bounced off him, without leaving a single mark behind. Oscar's knuckles split on Steele's stomach and first blood was drawn. The bloodthirsty crowd screamed its approval.

The smell of sweat and smoke was suffocating, even up in the ring where the two fighters battled. Steele punched his opponent square in the jaw and he watched silently, resignedly as Oscar went down on one knee. Steele had remembered that he must make it to the tenth round or his father would use the stick on him, and he'd pulled his punch at the last second. But he'd still hit the man with enough force to make it look good for the crowd.

Steele had honed his showmanship to a fine art. He'd had to, to survive the fickleness of the crowd who would turn on him in a second if he dared to show weakness.

Oscar rallied and began dancing around the ring. Steele followed his every move, careful to never let his opponent out of his sight. A few moments of this and the bell rang, signaling that the round was over.

Steele looked into the crowd, searching for his father. What caught his attention first was the strong, steady gaze of a tall, gray-haired man. The man was quieter than those surrounding him, barely moving. His gaze caught Steele's and held it fast.

Steele looked away, feeling strangely ashamed. Then, unable to resist, he looked back and found the man's gaze still solid upon him. He looked away again and caught sight of his father, waving around a fistful of cash, drunk on beer and the victory he felt sure was imminent.

Steele realized that the only thing keeping him in this ring was love for his father. Steele was still a child, even if he did have an adult's body. It was his fondest wish to make his father proud. But he knew, deep in his tortured heart, that his father would never love him in return. He'd long ago accepted that, but Steele still wanted to please him. Why? Even Steele knew his father certainly didn't deserve his devotion.

Steele clenched his jaw. He'd never been one to think such disloyal thoughts of the man who had sired him. He felt the gaze of the quiet, gray-haired man in the audience and knew that this stranger had something to do with it. He didn't have to look to know the man still watched him in that strange, quiet way. But he looked anyway.

Why was he doing this? Did he really fear his father's stick so much? It only hurt because his father wanted it to, bruising Steele's heart more than his body.

The second round began and Steele stepped into the center of the ring, suddenly resolute in what he was going to do. Oscar danced up to him and threw a wide punch that glanced off Steele's ear.

Steele took the dive and fell onto the mat with a crash. He stayed down, eyes closed, as the referee counted out the seconds to total knockout. As the man reached the count of ten, Steele opened his eyes a crack and saw the gray-haired man walking toward his father.

The match was over. A new victor had been named. Steele let himself be led off the stage, staggering and wincing for show. His father came up to him, yelling and sputtering in his rage. "Boy, you'd better explain why you threw that match."

"I didn't, Dad. He really beat me hard."

It was more than clear that his father didn't believe him. "When we get home I'll show you what a beating truly is."

Steele felt his stomach clench in fear and dread.

The gray-haired man reached them. "Mr. Steele, may I speak with you?"

"What do you want?" his father growled.

"I want your son."

Steele's father started, then laughed. "What, you want him for sex?"

The man never batted an eyelash. "No. I wish to train him for the big ring."

"Bullshit," his father spat.

"I want to take him off your hands for good. And I'm prepared to offer you a nice lump sum for the honor."

His father eyed the man warily. "How much? I wanna know how much you're offering."

"Fifty thousand dollars," the man replied flatly.

Steele's heart sank heavily.

"I'll take it," his father said. "The boy is useless to me now anyways."

"I don't want to go!" Steele pleaded with his father, already knowing the battle had been lost. Fifty thousand dollars was too good a price to turn down—even Steele knew that.

"Shut up boy," he said. "You better be glad this man— what's your name?"

"William Murdock."

"You'd better thank Mr. Murdock for saving you from the beating you so richly deserve."

"I can make a comeback," Steele swore. "Just give me one more chance Dad, please."

"Whether you can make a comeback or not doesn't matter to me anymore boy. You're soiled goods now. You've broken your winning streak. I don't have any use for you now."

Steele's eyes stung with tears as he watched his father and William Murdock talk over the particulars of his sale. He felt like an object, a slave to the cruel whims of fate. He didn't know what he would do with this William Murdock, this man who had no idea of his strange abilities. His dad knew of them, had always known.

Steele knew his new owner would have trouble believing him if he told him of his ability to withstand even a bullet at point-blank range without injury. He wasn't a normal boy by anyone's standards—especially when one took into account his incredible endurance and power. He had the strength of ten grown men—he could bench-press a Mini Cooper for goodness' sake. Steele was just a freak in a world populated with freaks, and what's more, he knew it.

A few minutes later, after the details had been worked out, his father left with a briefcase full of money, never once looking back at his son. Steele watched him go with a hopelessness that threatened to drown him. He felt Murdock move closer to him. "He would have taken half that much, you know," Steele murmured softly to his new owner.

"I know. But you're more than worth the money. Not to worry son, I'll take good care of you, you'll see. Your days of struggle are over."

"I threw that fight because I wanted out of boxing. And you want to train me for the 'big ring', as you called it? I don't want that, thank you very much, sir."

"That big ring I referred to is life," Murdock said gently. "I will train you to use your abilities to their fullest, and with training comes understanding. You'll know yourself at last, and you'll be safe in my care as you learn. I wish to prepare you for the world, my boy."

"What do you know of my abilities?"

"I've been watching you for some time now, Brian Steele. I know you're incredibly strong and capable of withstanding an enormous amount of damage with nary a qualm. You can deflect a barrage of blows without batting an eye, much less sustaining an injury. You can run for miles on end and never become winded. You could destroy a man with only one blow if you so choose. You're resilient in a way that I've never seen before, and I want to help you learn to use this to your advantage in every way."

Steele tried not to fall for Murdock's easy, gentle ways, but it was impossible. Steele's heart had already softened and his fear was fading.

"Come on. Let's leave this ruckus behind us forever," Murdock said, putting his arm about Steele's shoulders, taking him through the crowd. "Have you ever been to Cleveland?"

Steele shook his head and left in the care of his new guardian.

Chapter One
Many years later

෨

Marla Rivers looked about her, recognizing all the familiar comforts of her home. The coma had lasted a little over a year. But her mother had kept up the payments on her house, never giving up the hope that Marla would come back to herself. That Marla would, eventually, wake up.

It had taken almost six grueling months of physical therapy to regain her ability to walk. And even now, Marla often walked with a cane. But at last she was home again, released from the hospital, safe and sound after her long absence.

She ignored the flickering of light as she passed by a lamp. She'd learned it was best to ignore such things.

Everything was as she'd left it. Nothing had been disturbed. She knew she had her mother to thank for that. The sense of familiarity was comforting to her after months spent in a strange, sterile hospital room.

She put her luggage away, weak with exertion when she was done but determined not to let it hold her back in any way. She felt like taking a bath but knew it was too soon to test herself in the large garden tub alone. She might slip beneath the surface of the water and never come back up. For awhile, at least, she would be taking showers.

She plopped down on her sitting room couch before the television. The set flickered and came to life. Marla frowned. She hadn't touched the remote.

She imagined the television turning to her favorite station, a cartoon station, and right on cue the TV changed channels for her.

Marla gritted her teeth. This was yet another new skill she'd developed in her year of coma-sleep. She blinked and the television turned off abruptly. So many things had changed. *She* had changed. The coma had opened a Pandora's box in her mind. This trick with the television was only one of many odd quirks she'd discovered over the last six months.

There came a knock at her door. She wasn't expecting visitors, but she imagined her mother had come by to check up on her. She got up and went to open the door, startled to find two men, not her mother, standing on her porch. They were dressed professionally, in matching black suits and gray ties.

"Can I help you?" She frowned.

"Are you Marla Rivers?" one of them asked.

"I am."

"We're here to talk to you about your new…uh, abilities."

Marla sighed, leaning heavily on her cane. "Not more reporters."

"We're not reporters. We represent a party interested in your gifts. May we come in?"

Marla thought hard on it. Her first instinct was to tell them to go to hell, she was too tired to entertain them, but curiosity got the better of her and she nodded, stepping back to allow them into her house. She led them to her sitting room and plopped down on the couch, offering them two chairs opposite her. "What party do you represent then?" she asked.

"We work for an organization called Siren Corp. After learning about you in the papers and on the news, my employers have taken great interest in your abilities," the man told her, self importance lacing his words so that they grated over her ears.

"What sort of interest?" she asked.

"We are prepared to offer you a large sum of money for the privilege of studying your unique gifts."

Marla blinked. The lamplight flickered but she ignored it, conscious that the two men were carefully watching for just that sort of thing. "How much money?" she asked.

The man placed a briefcase on his lap and opened it, showing her the contents. "One hundred thousand dollars," he said.

Marla choked back a gasp as she saw all the money in the case. It was almost comical, the stereotypical case of money. She almost laughed but managed to control herself at the last second.

She could hardly believe her good fortune. She could really use that money. Her hospital bills were astronomical and she didn't want to rely on her mother so heavily now that she was home again, gracious though her mom had been in helping her. Marla no longer had a job, and this money would take a little of the pressure off while she looked for one.

She desperately needed the money. Marla feared that eventually the creditors would come harassing her and she might have to sell her beloved house just to get by.

But there was something about the two men's offer that bugged her. Something about *them* that made her uneasy. "What do you mean by 'studying' my gifts?" she asked at last.

The second man, quiet until now, spoke up. "We just mean to observe you, to see what triggers these gifts, what makes them work."

"Like a lab rat," she couldn't help pointing out.

"Don't make it sound so bad," he frowned. "It's a privilege, what we offer you. One many others would jump at the chance to accept."

Marla raised one eyebrow. "So go to these other people," she said, testing them.

It seemed that the two men wished to play good cop, bad cop with her and she didn't like it one bit. The first man spoke up again, playing the role of good cop. "Please don't dismiss this out of hand," he said evenly. "We will study you, it's true, but you'll be perfectly safe."

Marla instinctively disbelieved him. "I don't think so," she said at last, mourning the loss of the chance to earn some fast cash. "I'm sorry but I'll have to decline your offer."

The second man, the bad cop, spoke again. "You would do well to reconsider that decision."

Marla frowned, anger boiling just below the surface. "Why don't you both just leave now?"

The men rose, towering over her as she sat on the couch, but she was determined not to feel intimidated. This was her home, damn it, her own private domain, one she felt she deserved after all the long months spent in the hospital. She didn't want her first day at home marred by these two men with their strange offer and high-handed behavior.

"You will accept our offer and be grateful for it," the bad cop said with a sneer.

Marla rose as quickly as she could from her position on the couch. The lightbulb in a lamp on the table next to the couch exploded. The two men started as the glass shattered, but Marla refused to budge. "Get out," she said again, nearly growling the words.

The bad cop pushed his suit jacket back to reveal a gun nestled in a shoulder holster beneath his arm.

Marla felt her eyes grow wide with surprise and fear. "Are you threatening me?" she fumed.

"You will accept our offer, one way or the other. If we have to use a little force to convince you, so be it."

Marla, furious now, bared her teeth at them. "If you don't get out, I'll call the police."

The man pulled his gun on her, and the other moved to close the drapes on the window of the sitting room. Marla felt a thrill of fear mix with her anger and stood shocked as she watched them. She came to herself with a snap and dove for the phone sitting next to the sofa. She barely touched it when she felt the man press the muzzle of his gun to the side of her head.

"I don't think so," he said. "Put the phone down. Now, we're going to try this again. Will you come with us willingly or not? Either way you *are* coming with us."

There came a deafening crash as the door to her home slammed open.

A huge man stepped into the room. He was massive, at least six foot ten with three hundred pounds of pure muscle on him. His head was shaved bare and his cool gray eyes were piercing and bright. He looked like a giant in the confines of the room, an uncivilized brute in a slate gray suit.

He zeroed in on the man holding the gun to her head. "Let her go," came his gruff command.

"Steele," he sneered. "We were here first. She's ours."

"I think the lady has a different opinion. Let her go."

"Sterling scum! You and Ryan Murdock can go fuck yourselves."

"I won't tell you again. Let her go," said the giant.

The man hesitated, keeping the gun pressed to her temple. Marla took matters into her own hands. She knocked the hand holding the gun away with a hard swipe of her fist. She pushed the gunman back and rushed to stand by Steele.

"I think the lady has made her decision," Steele said, eyes never leaving the two men.

"This isn't over yet," the gunman growled. He and his colleague left with surly looks on their faces, passing close to Steele but not daring to touch him.

When they were gone, Marla discovered she'd been holding her breath and let out a huge sigh. She grabbed her forgotten cane from where it rested against the couch. She leaned on it for support as she felt her heart rate return to normal. "Now who are you and what made you think to break down my door?"

"I'm Brian Steele, but you can call me Steele. I work for a government project called Sterling. I came to meet you and noticed the Siren vehicle out front. I figured it was in both of our best interests to get in here and make sure you were all right."

His voice held such strength that Marla felt herself beginning to relax somewhat. Marla put a hand to her head, feeling a headache coming on as her ever-present fatigue pulled at her. She'd been prone to headaches recently as well as weakness. "Siren? What do you mean?"

"Those two men work for an outfit called Siren."

"How do you know that?"

"Because I've seen them before. And because I make it a point to know most of Siren's employees. Siren is an opposing project funded by an entirely different consortium of investors. While we at Sterling study the untapped resources of the human brain, Siren seeks to augment them with technologies that have no business being employed on any human."

"What do they want with me?" she asked.

"They wish to exploit your gifts. Exploit and manipulate them to their own ends."

She had suspected as much. "And what are *you* doing here exactly?"

"I'm here to ask much the same, but my intentions are honest, I assure you. Sterling is very interested in your gifts. We wish to study them, catalogue them, and perhaps help you to understand and therefore control them in time."

Marla shook her head in disbelief. "What makes you think I'll accept your offer when I wouldn't accept theirs? They offered me quite a handsome sum, you know. You haven't offered me anything yet."

Steele smiled, revealing a row of very white teeth. "You haven't given me a chance."

Marla couldn't help but respond to his smile. He was quite handsome when he smiled. And despite his massive size, she felt no instinctive fear of him as she had with the two men from

Siren. "So make an offer," she grinned, feeling the last of her lingering panic disappear.

"We're prepared to take care of all your medical bills incurred during your coma and recuperation. We'll also have our own doctors on staff to ensure your continued safety and well-being."

She grew dizzy and faint, and when her head stopped spinning she realized she was practically in Steele's arms. He was keeping her from falling with gentle and patient hands. Her heart fluttered with an excitement she hadn't felt in almost two years, as she felt the burn of his skin seep into hers. She was overly aware of his male magnetism, of his sheer strength and size. She wondered if he was this large all over. She shook her head as if to clear it of her wanton thoughts and eased her body away from him.

"'Aren't you going to offer me money straight up, as they did?" she asked weakly.

"How much do you want?" he returned.

"Are you serious?" She laughed tiredly.

"Absolutely."

She eyed him for several seconds. "What, so I can ask for a hundred thousand dollars and you'd give it to me?"

"How does a solid five hundred thousand sound?" he asked, deadpan.

Marla reeled. "I don't believe this." She clutched her aching head and stepped completely out of Steele's supportive arms, determined to stand on her own. She immediately, keenly felt the loss of his touch. "This is just too much for me."

"I could come back later, to give you some time to think it over."

"Are you crazy? I don't have to think! Of course I'll take your offer. I'd be insane not to. My medical bills alone will set you back something like a million dollars. Maybe more. I'll take your offer gladly."

Steele smiled again and her stomach did a strange little somersault. "Good. I'll leave you today to get your rest, but I'll be by in the morning to pick you up. How does nine o'clock sound?"

"It sounds great," she said.

"Be sure to lock your door after me, and don't answer it for strangers."

Marla nodded. She didn't have to be told twice. Steele gave her a small bow, turned and left the way he came, closing the door softly behind him. Marla moved to engage all three locks on her door and leaned heavily against it when she was done.

She'd been having weird days ever since awakening from her coma. But this was, by far, one of the weirdest she'd ever experienced.

Chapter Two

ജ

Later that evening, after the sun had sunk in the sky, Steele walked into Ryan Murdock's office without knocking. "I put two guards on her," he said without preamble. "Siren got to her first and scared her pretty badly. But she's agreed to come in with us."

Ryan pursed his lips. "I knew Siren would want her, but I didn't think they'd act so fast."

"It's no wonder. She's as strong as we believed. Maybe stronger. That's why Siren wasted no time in contacting her. But they made a huge mistake in trying to bully her. She may still be weak on the outside, but she's strong as stone on the inside. She didn't stop fighting, even when they backed her into a corner."

Ryan mulled over this. "They must want her pretty badly to try and force her like that so soon."

"My sentiments exactly," Steele replied.

"Keep a guard on her at all times when she's away from the compound. I don't want anything else to happen to her while she's under our care. The less stress she has, the better we'll be able to work with her."

"Siren will try again to get her," Steele pointed out.

"I know. The persistent bastards. But we'll just have to deal with that when the time comes."

There came a knock at Ryan's door. "That'll be Vicious." He reached out to hand Steele a manila folder. "Here's tonight's assignment."

Steele moved, file in hand, and opened the door. The dark-haired man on the other side gave Steele a nod as he passed out of the office, then took his place within. The door closed on the two men and Steele rubbed a hand over the top of his head.

It was time to shave again. He could feel persistent spikes of hair trying to grow. He hated his hair—a cross between red and blond, it curled like crazy and only served as a distraction when he was working. Enemies could easily grab one's hair and yank savagely. He couldn't—and wouldn't—have that.

He looked down at the file in his hand and opened it. Pictures of men stripping down stolen cars lay within, as well as a schematic of the building they were using to carry out their illegal activities. Steele clenched his jaw, shut the folder and went to prepare for the long night ahead of him, putting the last lingering thoughts of Marla aside.

* * * * *

Marla lay in bed, mind running furiously, keeping her from sleep. Night filled the room—she'd unplugged all of the electrical appliances—and a slight cool breeze came in from the open window. Oh how she'd missed the feel of fresh air washing over her skin!

She couldn't stop thinking about the events of the afternoon. Everything had changed for her within the space of a few minutes. If Steele was to be believed, and strangely enough she did believe him, then she needn't worry anymore about her hospital bills or her lack of a job. From near bankruptcy, she now had a fortune to look forward to.

All she had to do was allow Sterling to study her. And that couldn't be too bad, could it?

Her thoughts took a turn and, with a sliver of anxiety, she dwelled on the odd and dangerous behavior of the two men from Siren. They'd actually dared to pull a gun on her! She didn't know what to think about that. She'd been scared, of course she had, but she'd also felt assured that she could gain the upper hand. Would they have fired on her had they known of her daring? How badly did they want to study her—if studying her was all they wished to do, which she doubted?

Marla admitted to herself that she wasn't entirely surprised by the offers from both parties. She'd suspected that, once the headlines in the papers had revealed her new quirks, something like this would happen sooner or later. She just hadn't expected it so shortly after her release from the hospital.

And what to think of the giant, Steele? He was a hulking brute of a man...but she'd sensed gentleness in his nature right away, and she sure as certain liked him better than the men from Siren. His eyes, nearly silver they were so gray, had spoken volumes to her. She knew instinctively that she could trust him.

She rolled over in bed and tried once more to find rest.

Seconds later she heard a faint sound coming from the front of her house and froze. The sound came again, a rattling sound like that of a doorknob. Marla crawled out of bed and went to her window. She looked down from her second-story room and saw the dark figure of a man by her front door.

Her heart thundered as a thrill of fear took her. She flew over to her closet and rifled within it. She came out holding a baseball bat and steeled herself for what she knew she must do next.

She crept down the stairs, careful not to make a sound, careful not to stumble on her still unsteady legs. She went to the side of the door, leaning against the wall for support as her knees suddenly went weak. With a click, the last lock turned and the door opened inward. Marla hardened herself, locking her traitorous knees in anticipation.

The dark, shadowy figure stepped into the room.

Marla raised the bat over her head and brought it down on the man's shoulder. He went down with a bellow of outrage, flailing out at her. Marla raised the bat again, swung and missed.

But it was just as well. Another man came through the door, moving so fast he was a blur, and she could barely follow him with her gaze. She staggered, fear choking her. But instead of coming for her, the newcomer zeroed in on the fallen man sprawled on her parlor floor.

"I'm sorry about this, Ms. Rivers," the new man apologized. "I looked away for a second and there he was."

Marla went weak against the wall. "Who are you?"

"They call me Vicious, but you can call me Johnny. I'm from Sterling. I was supposed to be guarding you while you slept."

Marla's eyes went wide with surprise. "You're from Sterling?" she asked, dazed.

"Yes," he answered, lifting the intruder to his feet. "Now to see who Mr. Sneaky is here."

The intruder was dressed all in black, with a stocking cap pulled down over his face. Vicious tore the cap from his head and Marla was surprised to see one of the men from Siren standing there. "What the hell?"

"You're a persistent son of a bitch, aren't you?" Vicious shook the man by the nape of the neck. "Didn't the lady already tell you no?"

"You can't win every time, you Sterling bastard," he snarled.

Vicious laughed and shook him again. "Didn't your mother teach you that breaking and entering is a crime? Or was it that your mother didn't like you enough to teach you anything important like that?"

The man twisted in Vicious' grasp, but Vicious held fast.

"I'm sorry you had to witness this, Ms. Rivers. Why don't you head back to bed? I'll take care of this asshole, pardon my French."

Dazed, Marla nodded and trudged over to the stairs. Then turned resolutely back. "What had you hoped to accomplish here?" she asked the intruder.

"We contacted you first. You're our project," he sneered. "You just haven't accepted that yet."

"Well, you can rest assured that after your behavior today and tonight, I'll do my very best not to ever have anything to do with Siren." Marla turned and went upstairs, content that Vicious would take care of things for her. She didn't know what to think about having a guard from Sterling watching over her, but in this instance she was grateful.

It was a long time, however, before she found sleep. It wasn't until the first faint pink streaks of dawn were showing through her curtains that she finally dozed off and found peace. And, strangely enough, her dreams were filled with images of Brian Steele.

Chapter Three

છ્ય

Steele waited patiently while Marla prepared herself for her first day at Sterling. He looked at the pictures on her mantel and marveled at how lovely Marla was. She had been heavier before the coma, full of breast and hip, and where before she looked much like a woman unafraid of a good time, she now looked fragile and breakable.

She had lovely red hair, long and curling down around the middle of her back. Her eyes, a startling cross between blue and green, were wide and large on her face. Her nose was a pert button, her lips a fullness that begged to be kissed. She had a small overbite that gave her a gamine look, one he had already started to appreciate despite himself.

Marla came down the stairs and walked over to him, her purse clutched tightly in her hands. "Should I bring anything else?" she asked, suddenly looking nervous, as if she didn't know how to proceed.

"No. Sterling will provide you with anything you might need." He led her out of the house. "Come on," he said, directing her to his idling Expedition outside. She had to crawl up into the seat and ordinarily Steele would have helped her into the cab of the vehicle, except that he was afraid to touch her. Afraid of what he might do. She was too beautiful, too fragile still, to get close to. And he was a brute at best.

She let out a huge sigh as she settled back against the plush seat. "So what exactly do you have to do with Sterling?" she asked softly, eyes closed.

"The same thing as you."

She started. "You can mess with electricity?"

"No. But I have an ability, the same as you do. Sterling acquired me when I was only thirteen. Back when my boss' father was in charge. I've been with them ever since."

"Acquired you?"

"Yes." He refused to elaborate.

"What's your ability then?"

"I'm generally the strong guy at Sterling. I take care of all the grunt work. I guess you could say I'm tough as steel." He smiled wryly at his own use of words.

Marla digested that. "That doesn't seem like an unusual ability. I mean, no offense, but aren't there a lot of people with the same gift? I once saw a guy take a cannonball to the stomach."

"I'm not at all like that," he said, keeping his eyes firmly focused on the road as he drove. "I'm something more."

"What?"

"You'll find out soon enough. Now," he said, changing the subject, "are you ready for your first day at our compound?"

"I don't know. Ask me that later."

Steele saw her smile out of the corner of his eye, her overbite evident, and he tensed. He realized his cock had grown hard and he tamped down on the rush of desire he felt. He didn't know this woman. She was lovely, yes, but that didn't account for his suddenly powerful hunger for her, not entirely. He needed to maintain control. She looked as if she might break under too much pressure.

"How are you feeling?" he asked, and hoped she didn't notice how hoarse his voice had become.

"Good," she said. "I feel a little better every day."

"Sterling will help you feel even better. The scientists working there are really…uh…nice. You won't feel awkward or weird around them. They'll accept you, extraordinary gifts and all, you'll see. It's a good place, Sterling."

"I hope so," she sighed. "I didn't thank you for putting a guard on me last night. I really appreciate that."

"I had a feeling Siren wasn't through trying to get to you."

"I don't know what I would have done without Johnny."

"He's a good man, if a little confused," he said enigmatically. "I knew he wouldn't let anything happen to you."

Steele felt compelled to say more. "Don't worry about Siren anymore. Everything will be okay. Trust me."

Marla looked at him and he stared resolutely at the road. She smiled. "I'll try."

"I couldn't ask for more," he said softly.

They drove on in silence, heading for the Sterling compound at a swift pace.

* * * * *

Steele accompanied her to Ryan Murdock's office and then turned to leave. "Will you come and see me later?" she asked hurriedly. She didn't exactly know why she asked it, but she'd been at ease in his presence and she wanted more of that feeling.

It also helped that he was absolutely gorgeous.

He was so tall, she felt dwarfed by him. And not only was he tall, he was heavily built, like a football player. He shaved his head and it looked good on him. His eyes were a cool, silvery gray that seemed to see more than what was on the surface. He had the squarest jaw she'd ever seen. And his neck, corded with muscle, drove her to distraction.

"If you want me to," Steele said. "Maybe we can have lunch together?"

"That would be nice," she said, feeling like an awkward teenager.

"I'll see you later then." He turned and left her there.

Marla leaned on her cane and knocked on Ryan's door. He called for her to enter and she did. "Hello there," he said. "You must be the lovely Marla Rivers."

"Hi." The lights flickered wildly and Marla sighed. "I'm sorry. I don't know how to keep from doing that."

"That, my dear, is why you're here with us today." Ryan smiled and rose from his seat behind the massive mahogany desk.

"My name is Ryan Murdock. My father started this project some fifty years ago. I'm now in charge of Sterling's affairs."

"Steele said you were funded by the government."

"Absolutely. We study and catalogue people like you. Gifted people, with talents not unlike your own."

"Sounds interesting." She tried not to fidget under Ryan's deep blue gaze. He looked as if he could see straight into the center of her, as if he could uncover all of her secrets with but a look.

"You've made the best decision in coming here to us, Marla. We'll have your gifts figured out in no time, you'll see. And you'll be able to learn about them yourself in the doing. Come with me and I'll introduce you to the team of scientists I've assigned to your case."

Marla followed him from the room. They walked down a long corridor, one that reminded her of the hospital that had been her home for nearly two years. People passed them by, each nodding a hello to her and Ryan. One man in particular caught her attention—Johnny. Or Vicious. Whatever his name was. He was tall and dark and handsome, with pale green eyes and chocolate brown hair, still dressed in the long coat he'd worn last night when he'd guarded her. He winked at her rakishly as he passed and Marla couldn't help but smile.

"Pay no attention to Vicious. He's a devil, that one," Ryan said after noticing her interest in the passing man.

Ryan led Marla to an elevator, which took them deep into the bowels of the massive compound. Four levels below the ground they stopped and exited into another labyrinth of corridors and offices. Marla tried not to be overwhelmed by it all, but she couldn't help feeling a little awe.

"How will I ever find my way out of here?" she had to ask.

"You'll have an escort until you're used to the surroundings. Don't worry, we won't let you get lost," Ryan assured her.

He led her to a room and ushered her in.

Three men and two women in white lab coats greeted them.

"Marla, this is your team. They'll be working nonstop to help you understand and control your new abilities. This is Jeff, Mark, Richard, Alice and Deirdre."

Marla shook each of their hands in turn.

"Well," Ryan clapped his hands together, "I'll leave you all to it then."

Marla watched him go and felt a moment of panic. But it subsided as Deirdre came and put her arm about Marla's shoulder. "Don't worry. We'll take good care of you. Come, let me show you a little of what we'll be doing today."

* * * * *

Lunchtime came quickly for Marla and her team. The entire morning had been spent going through test after test. A CAT scan, a brainwave monitor and a urine test had been the first steps on the agenda. Marla didn't know what these tests would reveal to her new colleagues that hadn't already been revealed to her many doctors back at the hospital. But Jeff had been certain that they were already making progress.

Time had flown and now Marla looked forward to seeing Steele once more.

She made her way to the cafeteria with the rest of her team, ignoring the flickering of the lights as she entered the room and grabbing a tray of lunch, realizing that she was quite famished. She turned, bumping into someone's chest, and was jolted out of her musings. "Sorry," she said, and raised her eyes to meet Steele's cool gray gaze.

He smiled gently. "It's all right. How have you been faring?"

"So far, so good." She led them to a vacant table and they sat opposite each other. "They've done quite a few small tests so far. Just hooking me up to machines and covering me with electrodes, stuff like that."

"Ugh. I hate the electrode cream they use," Steele said.

Marla chuckled. "Me too."

They ate their lunches in a companionable silence for several minutes.

Marla almost hated to break the soothing silence. "So what do you do here? I've been told that you live here in the compound."

Steele nodded. "You've asked about me?"

Marla blushed.

A small smile played at the corner of Steele's mouth. "I've lived here since I was thirteen. I like it here. It's safe for a person like me."

"What about your parents?"

Steele's smile disappeared. "My mom died giving birth to me and my father...well, let's just say I don't miss him much."

"Oh. I'm sorry," she apologized.

"Don't worry about it. What about you? How are your parents faring after these new developments?"

"My mom is all I have, and she's nothing but supportive of me. She and I don't talk much about my new quirks, but we both know they're there. Without her help I never would have made it out of the hospital."

"I understand that your coma lasted a year," he said.

"Yeah, it was a long time. I lost most of my motor skills and had to relearn how to walk. It was hard work, but I had very determined physical therapists and they assured me I was recovering with great speed."

"How did you end up in the coma?" Steele asked.

Marla blushed. "I was putting a lightbulb into the ceiling fan at my house and I fell. It's not glamorous but there it is. I don't remember much. For me, no time passed from that fall—heck, I hardly remember the fall itself—to when I woke up in the hospital over a year later."

"That sounds frightening," he said.

"Only if I think about it." She shrugged with a grimace.

Her eyes drank in the sight of his delectable mouth as it twisted into a wry grin. "This place can help you heal," he said.

"I'm starting to believe you're right about that." She couldn't help a rush of desire as his beautiful eyes roved over her face, searching out the truth of her statement.

He cleared his throat and looked away, almost guiltily. "Uh, are you doing anything tonight?" he asked.

Marla's heart beat double time. "No."

"Would you like to have dinner with me?"

"I'd love it." She would.

Steele rose, grabbing his now empty tray. "If you'll still be here around six, I can come fetch you and take you back to my apartment. I'll make a meal you'll never forget."

Marla grinned. "That sounds lovely."

Steele nodded and turned, leaving her there.

She focused on her lunch, mind in a quandary as she thought back over the day's events. Between each thought was an image of Steele, taking her off guard. He was certainly handsome enough for her to daydream about, but she was far too old for such frivolous musings. She tried valiantly to push him away and concentrate instead on what lay ahead of her in the lab.

Johnny Vicious plopped down into Steele's vacated seat a few minutes later. "Hey there," he said.

Marla started and dropped her fork. Before it could land, Vicious' hand struck out — so fast she couldn't follow the movement with her eyes — and caught it neatly. She smiled at him, amazed at his speed. "Hey yourself."

"Sorry about last night."

"Don't worry about it. I'm over it now." She grinned. "So why are you here? What do you do for Sterling besides guard people like me?"

"I'm the result of an experiment gone bad," he laughed.

Marla started. "What do you mean?"

"I was part of a sleep deprivation study here and it didn't work out. Now I just do odd jobs for Sterling."

"Sounds fun I guess."

"It is," he countered, and grinned. "So I hear you're recovering from a coma and there are...complications, shall we say, brought on by your big sleep."

"You act as though you hear about people like me all the time."

"Around here you do." He smiled slyly. "I also see you've taken a liking to our big guy Steele."

Marla growled. "You're not a very nice man, are you, Johnny Vicious?"

"Oh I can be very nice when I want to be," he laughed.

Marla rose, but Vicious stopped her by reaching across the table to grab her arm. "I didn't mean to rile you," he said. "I just wanted to tell you that Steele is a good man. He's a true gentleman."

"Whereas you aren't?"

"Guilty." He jumped from his seat so fast that if Marla had blinked she would have missed the move. "Well, I'm off. Take care of yourself and the big guy, would you Marla? I like to think of Steele as a friend and I can already tell just by looking at you both together that you two need each other. Be good to him." He walked jauntily away, leaving her dumbfounded in his wake.

Chapter Four

ຂ⌒

Steele came around to pick her up from the lab at precisely six o'clock. He watched as Deirdre removed the last of the electrodes from Marla's temples, a strong, silent support that Marla greatly appreciated.

"We'll see you tomorrow at the same time," Mark called out as she rose and went to Steele.

"Yeah, I'll see you then." She waved goodbye to her team members and allowed Steele to lead her out of the room.

"I hope you like spaghetti," Steele told her, taking her down the winding corridors of the Sterling compound. "I make it from scratch."

Marla was impressed. "I don't think I've ever had spaghetti that didn't come straight from a box before."

"I like to cook. It gives me time to think," he said.

"I'm lucky if I can make toast without burning it," she chuckled.

Steele led her through hallway after hallway until Marla was completely disoriented. Finally they came to a door, which Steele opened and allowed her to step through first.

Steele's apartment was a working contrast against its owner. Where Steele was large and strong, much of his décor was delicate and homey. Marla walked into the sitting room and looked around. It was done in soft hues of vanilla and neutral beiges. It was a soothing room. Comfortable. And already the delicious smells of his still-cooking food were filling the air.

Marla noticed right away the several bonsai trees placed here and there about the room. "You practice bonsai?" she asked, surprised.

"I try. My hands are sometimes too big for it though," he replied softly.

The trees, so small and delicate, were lovely and she told him so. "How many do you have?"

"I just acquired my seventeenth."

It spoke volumes about him, that he took such great care of things so much more delicate than he was. "Wow. You've got a lot more patience than I do, that's for certain."

"I just like to know that I'm taking care of something that needs me," he said with a slight blush.

Marla thought his words and sentiment were beautiful. She took a deep breath of the air to steady her suddenly fraying nerves and smelled the wonderful aroma of the spaghetti. "That smells great." She sniffed again and smiled.

"This way." He took her deeper into the apartment. His kitchen, off the left side of the sitting room, was large for such a small apartment, with enough room for a small breakfast table within. Marla looked at the table, already set with delicately fine china and tall candlesticks.

"How lovely." She came forward to run her finger down the curve of a plate decorated with tiny orchids.

"Have a seat. I'll serve."

Marla watched as he took their plates and filled them with spaghetti. Once he was seated across from her she poured them each wine from a waiting bottle.

"You didn't have to go through all this trouble for me," she told him.

"I like having the excuse to go all out," he said softly. "Please," he motioned toward her plate, "eat."

The first bite nearly made Marla swoon. It was the best spaghetti she'd ever tasted by far. The noodles were absolute perfection and the sauce was tangy and sweet and amazing. "This is delicious."

"Thank you." He took a large bite himself.

The wine flowed freely as did the conversation. Before Marla knew it, it was going on nine o'clock. She'd been talking to him for almost three hours without feeling the time pass at all. Her head was fuzzy from the alcohol, but her senses were heightened. It was a lovely feeling.

She couldn't stop staring at Steele's lips. They kept distracting her. They looked soft and utterly kissable. She couldn't help but imagine how they would feel moving over hers. She looked away with a guilty start, only to be drawn back to looking seconds later.

"Do you have a girlfriend?" she asked him suddenly, and nearly kicked herself for being so blatantly interested.

Steele smiled as if he knew what was on her mind. "No," he replied gently.

"Why not?"

"My life is completely wrapped up in Sterling. Most women wouldn't understand that."

"Well, I'm not most women," she said boldly, watching him closely.

Steele rose to his feet and took her hand. He pulled her up from her seat with gallant care. "This is happening so fast," he whispered, and rested his forehead against hers.

"I know. But I like it," she said honestly.

"I didn't bring you here to ravish you."

"I know. But that doesn't mean you shouldn't anyway."

"You're still weak."

"I'll always be weak from that damn coma if I don't try to overcome it." She smiled. "I'm willing to try with you."

"I don't want to hurt you," he whispered, his warm breath fanning over her mouth.

"Then don't," she whispered back.

He brought his hands up to the sides of her temples. He gently ran his thumbs over her eyes, closing them. "I want to kiss you," he breathed.

"Yes," she gasped, in thrall to his touch and his nearness. "Yes."

He cradled her head in his hands and slowly, as if to give her time to turn away, he lowered his mouth to hers. The first contact of their lips touching made her heart thunder a tempestuous rhythm. His mouth was the softest she'd ever kissed. Marla put her arms around his neck and pulled him closer.

His big hands were so gentle, holding her captive to his kiss. She sank into the embrace and felt heat pool low in her belly. She let her hands slide down over the bulging ridge of muscles that were his chest and opened her mouth to his questing tongue, gasping when he gave it to her.

The flavor of him blossomed on her tongue. He tasted of spice and wine and man. He put his arms around her and held her tight against him so that Marla could feel the enormous ridge of his erection.

Everything on his body was built on a surprisingly large scale.

His big, broad palm pressed into the small of her back, bringing her even closer against him. His tongue slid alongside hers, his lips moving over hers until she was mindless to anything else. She kneaded the muscles of his chest then moved her hands lower, over his belly.

Steele sucked in a deep breath and pulled her hands away. "Don't. I'm ticklish," he murmured against her mouth. Marla filed that information away for later inspection.

He lifted her easily up in his arms, holding her so that her feet dangled inches off the floor. "I can't stop," he breathed.

"Don't," she gasped into his kiss. "Whatever you do, don't stop."

She ran her hands over the stubble on his scalp and held him tight to her. Steele's mouth moved over her jaw and down to her throat. Marla let her head fall back as he kissed her, offering herself to him completely, holding nothing back.

Marla's hands found their way beneath his shirt and she was astonished at how tightly muscled he was. His clothes did him little justice, hiding all this wonderful flesh from view. She pushed his shirt up and he set her down and removed it the rest of the way himself. Marla pulled off her own shirt, leaving her bra between them. Steele then scooped her back up in his arms and let his mouth move over her collarbone with hot intensity.

Steele carried her out of the kitchen and into his bedroom. An enormous California king-sized bed waited for them in the center of the room. Steele laid her down upon it with gentle care and looked at her intently. "Do you want this, Marla?" he asked, giving her one more opportunity to back out.

"Yes," she gasped, reaching for him.

Steele caught one of her hands and pressed a hot kiss to the center of her palm. "Tell me if I'm going too fast for you."

Marla moaned and arched up to him as he came down upon her on the bed. He fanned her hair out on the pillow, positioning each lock just so until he was satisfied with it. He straddled her and his hands went to the front clasp of her bra and released it. Her breasts spilled free and he was there to catch them, cupping them tenderly in his hands, kneading and stroking them until she gasped.

Her nipples were hard and long, swollen with the need for his touch. He pulled at them teasingly with his fingertips, rubbing and stroking them like she suddenly longed to rub and stroke his cock. His mouth came down and covered her there, burning her with the heat of his kiss and she gasped, arching into his caress. His hand covered her other breast as he suckled her, kneading and plumping it over and over with his huge palm and strong fingertips.

His hand moved down over her body, onto the slight swell of her stomach, and he petted her there like he might a kitten. His fingers tangled on the fastening to her jeans and her breath caught behind her suddenly parched lips. The button gave way, then the zipper, and Steele slid his hand into the waistband of her panties.

He covered the mound of her sex with his hand. His long fingers curled down, cupping her fully, and he spread the lips of her pussy wide. The tips of his large fingers dipped into her wetness and spread it up to her clit. He rubbed the small nub of flesh and lightning seemed to arc through her at the touch.

The lights in the bedroom flickered then went out. The bulbs had blown, leaving them in total darkness.

Marla gasped for air. "Sorry," she apologized for the startling interruption.

"It's all right," he soothed, chuckling softly and still gently stroking that wicked finger over the swell of her clit. His mouth sucked hard upon her nipple then released it with a wet popping noise. He moved his lips over to her other breast and she forgot all about the lights.

Steele leaned back and stripped her pants from her legs. He spread her legs wide and lowered his body between them. His fingers wandered beneath the crotch of her panties and he was stroking her clit again, making her gasp.

"You're so wet," he growled.

And Steele was so hard he felt like a stone giant as he loomed over her in the bed. But Marla reveled in his obvious strength, her hands kneading the bulging muscles of his biceps, filling her hands with the intoxicating feel of his power.

He moved down her body, his lips trailing from her breast to her belly to her hip. His fingers pushed the crotch of her panties aside further and then his mouth covered her.

Marla cried out her surprise and it turned into a moan as his skillful tongue darted out to lap at her clit. As he gave her his most sensual kiss, he brought both of her legs up over his shoulders, opening her even more fully to his caress, making her feel vulnerable and small in the face of his sheer strength and overwhelming size.

His lips and tongue played with her, teasing her, tempting her. She grew impossibly wetter beneath his touch. He suckled the outer lips of her labia, making soft, wet noises with his mouth against her, and his fingers stroked her slit over and over until she was sobbing for breath.

Steele rose up over her and took her hands. He sat back on his feet and pulled her astride his hips. Marla's fingers caught the clasp of his jeans and made short work of undoing it. He was wearing briefs, which Marla pushed down, and his enormous cock fell like a weight into her hands.

He was incredibly well endowed, that much was obvious. Marla had never seen a cock so large, so thick, so long and wide. His skin was smooth and he was uncircumcised so that his foreskin was like a silken blanket around his sex. She stroked him from tip to base and back again, marveling at the beauty of him, and watched as a droplet of pre cum wept out of the opening in his penis.

Steele pushed her back gently and removed his pants and briefs. He then tore her panties from her and brought her back astride him. He leaned back and positioned his cock at the opening of her pussy.

He caught her gaze with his. "There's no turning back now," he said, and slid slowly into her.

Her body, unaccustomed to the invasion of his, tightened as he filled her. She felt stretched, burned by his cock, but it was a feeling she reveled in and welcomed more of as he entered her inch by thick, delicious inch. His body was so hot against hers that she was soon perspiring, as was he. Their bodies slid against each other, moist and smelling of spicy, sweet sex.

He was only halfway inside her when her body suddenly clamped down upon his. She came softly with a shudder as he held her gently against him. Her body milked his, trembling and squeezing around his cock until they were both gasping for air.

When it was over, Steele pressed further into her. He was so large and so strong, but he was gentle as a spring rain in the way he handled her. He demanded no more than her body was willing to give him, sliding to the heart of her with easy patience and care.

He put his hands beneath her bottom and brought her closer against him. Her legs spread wider about his hips and she hooked her ankles behind his waist for leverage. She gasped and trembled, her body still in that post-coital world that she hadn't experienced in over two years, and he held her tenderly until she eased against him once more.

Steele lifted her easily with his hands and brought her back down. He did all the work, helping her to ride him with nothing but his incredible strength. She slid up and down on his cock, her body making soft, wet sucking noises with every movement they made together.

Her nipples scraped against his chest and he lifted her so that his mouth could suckle her there. His teeth scraped against her tender flesh and she cried out, clutching him to her. His lips drew on her like a babe, pulling at her nipples until they were long and hard as diamonds.

His hands were at her waist, lifting and lowering her on his dick, but they were gentle and light, as if he were still affording her the opportunity to pull back.

No way in hell was she stopping things now. She'd never felt so alive, so powerful and beautiful as she did in Steele's muscular arms. Her long hair cocooned them and Marla rested her forehead against Steele's, lips aching for his kiss. He took her mouth as he took her body, softly, gently and tenderly. His tongue slid in alongside hers, filling her with the wild and untamed flavor of him.

Marla's body drew tight on the wrack of pleasure. She fought to move faster on him, but Steele held her steady and sure in his arms. Marla gasped and tore her mouth away from his. "Please," she begged, not even knowing what she was begging for.

The lights beyond the room flickered wildly.

Steele's body surged up into hers, balls deep, and Marla cried out her surprise. He moved her faster upon him, harder and deeper, until she was sobbing for breath. His hands squeezed the cheeks of her ass and she moaned. One of his fingers traced the cleft of her bottom and she was lost.

Marla came again with a tiny scream that was silenced by Steele's mouth. She quivered in his arms, seeing bright pinpoints of light like stars behind her tightly shut eyelids. Her body unraveled, the wave of release too great to withstand. She screamed again and fell limply against his massive chest, gasping for air.

The lights beyond the room flickered wildly.

Steele pounded into her, hard, harder and then he too found the bright climax, groaning his satisfaction aloud like a mighty jungle cat. His cock swelled and pulsed inside her cunt, spurting his cum deep inside the heart of her until she was wet and burning with his juices.

When their breathing had calmed, Steele reached up and tucked an errant stand of hair behind her ear. "Did I hurt you?" he asked.

Marla smiled blissfully and nuzzled his neck. "Not at all."

"God you make me feel so good." He pressed a kiss to her temple and held her tight against him.

"Me too. I haven't felt this good in...well, I can't even remember," she admitted with a laugh.

From somewhere beyond the bedroom Marla heard a clock strike eleven. "I need to get home and get some sleep if I'm going to be worth anything tomorrow."

"You could always stay here," Steele offered hopefully.

Marla shook her head. "I have to go home. I need a change of clothes and my medication."

Steele grunted. "Let's get dressed then and I'll take you home."

Getting dressed was much harder to do with Steele's hands roaming over her body every other breath, but somehow Marla managed. Then it was her turn to stroke his body as he dressed, roving her hands all over him. It was fun to play and unwind after a hard day...and a hard ride.

Marla gathered her things and followed Steele out of his quarters. She still wasn't used to all the winding corridors of the Sterling compound, but she was learning fast. They made it out to the parking lot where Steele's Expedition waited in less than five minutes. Steele gallantly helped her up into the cab of the vehicle, his hand lingering on her arm.

"I'm not a man who can tolerate a one-night stand."

"Me either. I mean," she amended quickly, "I'm not a *woman* who can tolerate a one-night stand either." She grinned.

He closed her door and walked around the vehicle to enter on the driver's side. His silvery gray gaze burned her, roving from her head to her toes, lingering on her lips, breasts and sex. Marla blushed and ate him up with her own eyes in return.

"Will you stay with me tomorrow night?" he asked softly. "I'll make us some steaks and baked potatoes. And after...we can do whatever you like."

Marla smiled. "Yes. I'd very much enjoy that."

Steele reached over and took her hand in his, not letting go until they pulled up in front of her house.

Chapter Five

ᛒᏫ

Steele helped her down out of the vehicle. When she was on her feet, he held her close to his heart. Marla hugged him back, feeling safer now than she had ever since waking up with one year of her life lost forever.

She stirred against him. "Why didn't you help me into the truck this morning?"

Steele chuckled softly. "I was afraid of what I'd do if I touched you," he admitted.

Marla blushed. "I see. Well, I'm glad you feel more comfortable touching me now," she laughed.

"Comfort has nothing to do with it." His gaze burned and he rubbed his erection against her belly. "I do love to touch you though." He stroked his hand down her back, his hand so wide and large that it nearly spanned her entire back.

Steele walked her up to the front porch, lingering as they reached it. He bent down and kissed her, his tongue delving deep. He pulled her into his arms, lifting her feet off the ground, and held her tight, his lips demanding on hers, as if he would never let her go.

He set her back down on her feet and pressed one last lingering kiss to her lips. "If I don't leave now, you won't get any sleep tonight."

His wicked promise made her knees turn to water and she leaned against him to keep from falling. He steadied her then turned to go. Dazed, euphoric, Marla turned to go into the house.

The door opened with nothing more than a push. She must have forgotten to lock it, though she'd never forgotten it before.

She hated having such a short memory for ordinary things like this. More than likely, she'd be feeling these aftereffects of her coma for the rest of her life. It was a depressing thought.

All this was happening just because she'd tried to change a lightbulb. It sickened her how easily she'd been brought low by a simple fall.

She turned on a light in her living room and gave a loud scream when she saw the man waiting there for her. Marla backed up, wanting to distance herself from the stranger standing in her home as though he owned it. The man watched her and slowly put his hand beneath the suit coat he wore. He pulled out an impressive-looking gun—big and silver, it glinted in the dim light—and pointed it at her.

"Have a seat, Ms. Rivers," he said softly, menacingly.

Marla plunked limply down on her couch, keeping her eyes focused on the gun at all times. "Who are you?"

"I'm Daniel Press, the acting junior director of Siren Corp."

Marla felt her eyes go wide. "I thought I'd seen the last of you people?"

"I decided to try and persuade you, personally, one more time to allow us to study you." His teeth glinted in the light. A razor blade smile. The smile of a predator.

"I've already told you no. My answer hasn't changed," she said bravely, feeling anything but. "A gun isn't going to make me change my mind, either."

"I could shoot you."

"Killing me isn't going to help you understand my quirks."

"Who said anything about killing you?" He fired the gun at her feet and she jumped up on the couch with a shriek, the explosion ringing in her ears. "The next bullet will be in your kneecap. You can count on it. I'm an excellent shot and we've doctors on standby in case it becomes necessary."

Marla's heart went cold with fear.

There came a sound at her door. "Marla? You forgot your purse in—" Steele halted mid-sentence as he saw Daniel. Daniel, surprised by the interruption, squeezed the trigger of the gun, pointing it squarely at Steele. Marla screamed at him to move, but it was too late. The gun went off with another mighty roar.

Steele didn't even flinch. He stood there and took the shot, unafraid of any damage it might cause. Miraculously, magically, it didn't cause him any harm at all. The bullet bounced off him, the slug falling uselessly to the floor at his feet.

Marla's jaw dropped in shock. The light in the ceiling blew with a loud popping noise in the sudden stillness, plunging the room into a shadowy darkness.

"Damn it, Steele. Don't interfere. This isn't any of your concern." Daniel growled from the shadows.

Steele ignored him and stepped further into the room, reaching Marla's side and stepping protectively in front of her. Daniel had the gun trained on them as they stood together united against him. "I beg to differ. She's working with us now. Leave her be. We both know you don't want blood on your hands over this."

"One day, Steele, I'm going to find a way to hurt you. And when I do..." He made a dramatic slicing motion across his throat.

Daniel kept the gun trained on them as he walked around them to the door. Steele reached out and snatched the gun from his hand, crunching it in his fists. Marla watched with disbelief.

Daniel suddenly screamed and clutched his head. He fell to the floor, writhing in agony. "Stop it," he shrieked. "Stop it Marla!"

Marla looked at Steele and shook her head. She had no idea what she was doing, if she was indeed doing anything at all.

Daniel choked out a scream, grasping his head in his fisted hands. Steele walked over to him, bent down and pried open one of Daniel's eyelids. "He's not faking," Steele said, looking back at Marla.

"Of course I'm not faking," Daniel spat unevenly, groaning.

Steele lifted him by the collar of his shirt and dragged him out onto the front lawn. Once there, Daniel seemed to ease, but the moment Marla stepped out onto her porch, he clutched at his head again with another agonized scream. Steele took Daniel's head in his own hands and carefully looked through his hair.

Steele pinched something off Daniel's scalp and held it up to the moonlight. Immediately Daniel eased, shuddering quietly on the ground.

"What is it?" Marla had to ask.

"It looks like a microchip," Steele said. "You must have interfered with it somehow. No wonder Siren wants you so badly." He grabbed Daniel's collar again and put his face close to the weakened man's. "What is this thing for?"

Daniel spat in his face.

Steele shook him. "You'll tell me what this is for one way or another. Choose wisely."

Daniel sobbed for breath. "It's top secret. You can't have the technology."

"I don't want the technology. But you'll tell me what it's for and quit stalling."

"It's a cerebral enhancing chip," Daniel said at last. "It's meant to improve motor skills and brain power."

"How does it work? It's not surgically implanted—how *can* it work?"

"It doesn't need to be implanted surgically."

"So what do you do, just plant them on people willy-nilly?" Marla asked, incredulous.

"Absolutely. We can put them on anyone," Daniel said with a smug smile.

"And you're testing this thing on humans? On yourself? Do your financial backers in the White House know what you're up to?"

"We've gone beyond testing. We have outfitted over a dozen men and women with the chip. And as for the government, they're on a need-to-know basis only, you know that from your own work at Sterling," he said slyly. He turned to look at Marla. "Did you know that the big guy here is a vigilante? He goes out almost every night to find the so-called bad guys and dispose of them one way or another."

Marla looked at Steele for confirmation of this shocking news.

"I've never killed anyone," Steele said softly. "And everyone I've helped to put behind bars richly deserved it, believe me. All I do is aid the police a little, whether they know it or not. I help them catch criminals red-handed."

Daniel smirked. "How noble you make it sound, when you're nothing more than hired muscle."

A car drove slowly down the road and Daniel leapt to his feet and bolted. Steele followed him easily, his long legs eating up the distance that Daniel's head start had given him. The car swerved as if the driver intended to run Steele down.

A split second before the car struck him, Steele brought his fist down on the hood. The car halted abruptly and nearly flipped over. Steele took his fist off the car, leaving an incredible dent behind. The driver got out of the car and ran down the street as fast as his legs would carry him. With one last murderous look at Steele, Daniel turned to follow his friend at a sprint.

Steele looked back at Marla. "I'm sorry," he said.

"Why?" she asked shakily.

"I didn't want you to ever have to see that."

"What, Siren?"

"No. My…uh…" He gestured to the smoking wreck of a car in the middle of the road. "My gifts. My curse."

Marla smiled and ran to him, throwing herself into his arms. He lifted her and held her close. "I'm glad you were here. I'm glad you're gifted. It makes me feel less alone in this world."

"You'll never be alone," Steele said thickly. "Never as long as I'm here."

"That was pretty amazing stuff," she said, marveling at how incredibly strong Steele was. Stronger than steel he might be, but he'd been nothing but gentle with her from the start. He was her own gentle giant. Her mighty protector.

Steele set her back down on the ground and looked at the microchip still held within his hand. "Ryan will want to see this."

"Let's take it to him."

Steele's gaze burned hers. "Not yet. It's late. And first I want to make sure you're okay."

Marla nodded. "I'm fine. Just a little shaken."

Steele swept her up in his arms like he would a babe and carried her back toward her house. "I need to see you naked, to make sure you're not injured in any way."

"Oh God, what will the neighbors think?" she giggled.

"I meant that I'll get you naked *inside* the house." Steele's mouth turned up at the corner in an endearing lopsided grin.

They crossed the threshold and Steele closed the door behind them.

* * * * *

The moment Steele set her down on her feet in the bedroom he began to strip her clothes from her body. Marla knew she wasn't injured but she let him have his way. He seemed determined to know for himself that she was all right.

Desire stirred in her blood and her breath caught.

Steele removed her bra and her breasts were bare to the cool night air. Her nipples were long and hard and aching for his touch. For his fingers and his mouth and anything else he wanted to put there.

When she was totally nude before him, Steele inspected her from head to toe. He found no injuries and let out a long, relieved breath. Then he seemed to realize that she was nude and his hands brought her closer to him.

Marla wanted him so badly her teeth ached. She went to her knees before him and reached for the fastening of his jeans. Her fingers fumbled. Steele growled and pushed her hands aside, making short work of the fastening himself and divesting himself of all his other clothes in record time.

His cock bobbed heavily between his legs, full and thick and hard with need for her. Marla pumped him, marveling at the way his foreskin moved over his beautiful penis. She pushed the skin back and laid her lips against the crown of him and he shuddered against her.

She let the head slip between her lips, opening wide to take him. Her tongue stroked him, tasting the tiny droplets of pre cum. She suckled softly, gently, and cupped his sac in one hand while the other masturbated him into her mouth. Her head bobbed over him and he pushed her hair back away from her face so he could watch her as she sucked him off.

Marla let one of her hands move down to her pussy, finding it moist and wet with desire. She found her clit and rubbed it the way she liked best. She put her fingers inside of her cunt, thrusting in and out the way she wanted his enormous cock to thrust in and out of her.

Steele pushed her away. "Not yet," he growled. He pushed her back onto the floor and came upon her, towering over her in the shadows. He spread her legs wide and brought his face down to her pussy. He let a long, silvery line of spit trail down onto her sex and Marla bucked beneath him, feeling the wetness sliding down her slit like the caress of a finger.

He positioned his massive cock at her opening and, without warning, thrust balls deep into her. He impaled her, hard into the heart of her, over and over. Her breasts bounced with their efforts and his hands came up to cup them lovingly.

Marla pushed him away after several thrusts and made him lie back on the floor. She moved down over him again and took his cock as deep into her mouth as she could. She tasted herself mixed with his spicy masculine flavor and she loved it. She licked him clean, sucking him, letting his cock go with a wet popping noise.

She straddled him, coming down over his cock, letting it fill her like a fist knocking at her womb. She rode him as she would a bucking bronco, moving her hips over him like the graceful movement of water, washing over him, taking all he had to give. She ground her pelvis against his, bouncing gently up and down upon him, squeezing her clit between their bodies as she fucked him. Steele leaned up, sending his cock even deeper into her, and took one of her nipples between his teeth.

He pushed her back, pulling free of her body with a wet, sucking sound and positioned her on her hands and knees before him. He mounted her from behind, balls slapping her tender flesh as he slid home. He held her shoulders and thrust into her again and again. He slapped her bottom until it stung, and she cried out as blindingly intense ecstasy washed through her body.

"Put your finger in my ass," she gasped.

Steele put his thick middle finger in his mouth and wet it thoroughly with his saliva. He then gently inserted it into her anus, turning it this way and that in time with the strokes of his cock into her pussy. He rode her that way, so gentle and yet so demanding, until she was gasping and begging for mercy.

Marla put her hand back on her pussy, spreading herself wide. She laid her head on the floor so that her bottom was high, high over her head, fully opening herself to Steele's pounding cock. She found her clit with her fingers and stroked over the hard nubbin of tender flesh.

Steele removed his finger from her bottom and took her hips in his hands, bringing her harder against his pelvic thrusts. Their bodies made wet, slapping noises together and the smell of their sex permeated the room. Marla had tears coming out of the corners of her eyes, and she moaned with every stroke Steele's body made inside of hers.

Steele abruptly pulled out of her. He bent down low behind her and put his mouth on her anus. He licked her there, his tongue a wicked weapon against her frazzling nerve endings. He thrust his fingers into her pussy and let her ride his hand for a moment as he licked and suckled and kissed her most forbidden flesh.

Minutes — what felt like hours — passed. The only sounds in the room were of Marla's weak, breathless moans and Steele's mouth kissing her anus. He rose up over her again and mounted her once more, stretching her wider than she'd ever been stretched before.

With a wild, keening cry, Marla came. Her body clamped down like a vise on Steele's enormous member. Steele groaned and found his own release, filling her pussy up with his creamy cum. Marla fell forward, limp, onto the floor. Steele rode her for a few more strokes and then stilled.

He stirred against her, pulling out. He turned her over onto her back and spread her legs once more. He put his mouth on her cunt, his tongue spearing deep into her pussy. His lips and teeth tugged at her clit and Marla was mindless with the endless sensations he visited upon her.

Impossibly, she came again, shuddering against his mouth and around his tongue. When it was over, when her breathing had calmed once more, Steele picked her up and laid her on the bed. He joined her seconds later and took her into his arms beneath the covers. They dozed, then fell deeply asleep, holding tight to each other.

It was the best sleep Marla had had in years.

Chapter Six
Two days later

&

"We've sent the chip in for analysis and I've informed my contacts of Siren's activities. Siren's been engaging in illegal activities for too long. Once their secrets are uncovered they shouldn't bother Marla anymore."

Steele nodded. "She's going to move in with me anyway. She just doesn't know it yet," he chuckled ruefully.

Ryan smiled. "I'm glad to see you so happy, Steele." He sighed. "I remember when Dad brought you here, that first day, when you were still so painfully shy about using your gifts. I remember envying you your strength because I knew the ladies really got into that sort of thing." He chuckled.

"I never knew that," Steele said. "I was too busy fighting my own nature, I think, to notice what was going on around me."

"When I found out you were so strong because of your mastery over your own Chi, I nearly ran myself ragged trying to do the same myself. It never worked." Ryan grinned sheepishly.

"I don't even know how I use my Chi. I doubt I ever will. But I was so grateful when my team of scientists told me that's what I'd been doing over the years—honing my life energy into something tangible and strong. That was when I first started to relax around here."

"I remember it took you awhile to grow accustomed to our way of life here."

"Your dad was the only real father figure I ever knew."

"I know."

"He bought me from my real dad, did he tell you that? For fifty thousand dollars."

"Yes. Years after you came here he told me," Ryan admitted.

"That was the best day of my life. I'll always be grateful to Sterling and to your father for helping me lead a normal life." The corner of his mouth lifted. "Well, as normal as it can be anyway."

"There's nothing to be grateful for, Steele. You're one of the best men I've got. Without you I don't think we'd be successful. You're very important to us."

Steele nodded. "I've got to get back. Marla will be through with her tests soon."

"How is she coming along?"

Steele shrugged. "She's not learning too much about why she obtained these powers of hers during her coma. But I think her team is coming up with a way to help her control them to some extent."

Ryan smiled. "She's a unique individual. We'll be happy to learn more about her and her new talents."

"So will we," Steele said, speaking of himself and Marla. "Marla's tired of sleeping with all the appliances unplugged."

Ryan and Steele shared a laugh over that.

There came a knock at the door and Johnny Vicious poked his head in. "Can I interrupt you two?"

"Sure, Vicious, what's going on?" Ryan asked.

Vicious looked at Steele. "Marla's doing some amazing stuff in the lab. I thought you might like to come and see for yourself."

Steele was on his feet in a second, followed by Ryan. The three men made their way over to the lab where Marla was running through her daily regimen of tests. Lights flickered along the way, some bulbs popping and going completely dark.

The closer they got to the lab the more chaotic the electrical bursts got.

There was a large window before the lab and Steele watched through it as Marla, strapped down to a chair, tossed her head back and forth. The machines she was hooked up to were going haywire, some smoking as they broke down completely. Her team of scientists was scrambling to protect their computer equipment, trying and failing to move the machines out of Marla's range.

All the lights in the compound went dark, flickered, then came back on. One of the scientists attached what looked like a rubber bracelet onto Marla's wrist. Then…silence. Stillness. The crisis was over, it seemed.

"That's amazing," Ryan breathed. "Truly amazing."

"You should have seen her a few minutes ago. She was arcing electricity from her fingertips to the computer towers." Vicious chuckled. "It was really pretty to watch."

Steele went into the room and immediately went to Marla's side. "Are you all right?" he asked.

Marla, shaken but still strong, nodded. "I'll be fine in a minute," she gasped.

Steele pressed a hard kiss to her mouth then turned to face the group of scientists huddled further into the room. "She's done here for the day," he said commandingly.

"Steele, it's okay. I'll be fine," Marla protested.

His silver gaze bored a hole into her. "You're. Done. Here. For. The. Day," he said firmly, enunciating each word carefully.

Marla let out a soft protest as Steele scooped her up into his arms. He carried her from the room, ignoring Ryan and Vicious as he passed, and took her to his apartment without stopping along the way.

He set her down on her feet, then took her hand and half dragged her into the bedroom. Steele looked down at her wrist, at the black bracelet that encircled it. "What's this?" he asked.

"It's a ground. Mark thinks it will help stop my outbursts," Marla answered. "I think he might be right. When I wear it the lights don't flicker anymore. I figure it's worth a try."

Steele nodded. "Get undressed," he commanded softly.

Marla blinked. "What, right now?"

"Yes, right now. Get naked. Or I'll do it for you and I don't trust myself to do that quite yet. You scared the hell out of me back there."

Marla felt her eyes go wide as he stalked her, towering over her.

"I'm going to give you the ride of your life," Steele promised, voice wicked and determined.

* * * * *

Marla was completely nude. And nervous. It usually didn't bother her, being naked, but this time Steele kept his clothes on. She didn't like to be a solo act.

"I don't trust myself yet," he whispered, when she begged him to take off his clothes.

He unbuttoned his pants and let his cock spring free. It seemed so much larger to Marla's wide, hungry eyes. She watched as he came close to where she reclined on the bed. "I want you to touch yourself," he said. "And I want you to watch me while you do it."

Marla put her hands between her legs and began stroking all over her sex. She spread the lips of her pussy wide for Steele's gaze, which blazed a trail over her naked body like a burning flame. She watched as he palmed his cock and began to stroke himself in time with her own movements.

"Suck your nipples," Steele commanded raggedly, his movements growing faster, more urgent.

Marla lifted her breast to her own mouth and let her tongue dart out to taste its peak. Steele groaned and pumped himself rapidly, his breath catching with each lick she gave her nipple.

She popped one into her mouth and sucked. Her other hand diddled with her clit, rubbing and squeezing it until she was bucking on the bed.

Steele groaned long and loud and came hard. His cum spurted onto her breasts and belly, and she rubbed the essence of him into her skin, reveling in the purely masculine scent of his release. He shuddered and put his still-spurting cock against her lips. She opened her mouth and tasted him, swallowing every last drop he had to give.

He tasted like magic. Sweet and spicy and delicious.

Steele came down upon her on the bed. He shoved his cock into the heart of her and began to ride her at a fast, breathtaking pace. He thrust harder and harder into her until the bed was squeaking and groaning from the abuse.

His fingers found her clit and squeezed it like she squeezed his cock with her body. Marla cried out and came explosively beneath his bucking body. Her pussy milked his dick, clamping down so hard that they both saw stars and lost their breath.

Steele took her ankles in his hands and pushed them up by her ears. He sank deeper, impossibly deeper, into the wet, welcoming heat of her body. Marla screamed and bucked beneath him, coming again and again. She was so wet her juices dripped to the covers beneath them. She was so hot her body felt as if it were on fire.

"Give me a baby, Marla," Steele groaned. "Take all of me."

Marla cried out. He thrust harder into her, nearly bruising her he loved her so savagely. The iron bar of him reached to the heart of her and filled her up with unimaginable passion, until she almost swooned with the rioting sensations that gripped her.

His hands held her ankles tight, never allowing her a chance to escape. As if she would have tried. She'd never felt so mastered, so completely split open and naked and vulnerable. He reached down with his hands and squeezed the cheeks of her ass. He slapped them hard, so that they stung, and the pain made the pleasure all the sweeter.

Marla came with a long groan. Her body shook beneath his and he rode her through the storm of her climax, thrusting deep over and over straight into her womb.

He shuddered and came seconds later, filling her with hot, scalding splashes of cum. Marla felt him burning inside of her, pulsing and hard and hot. He filled her up until she was overflowing with his essence. His mouth came crashing onto hers and seconds later his body followed, taking her down deep into the mattress.

"I love you Marla," he said hoarsely at her ear.

Marla felt her eyes tear up. "I love you too Steele. With all my heart."

He kissed her one last time and they both fell asleep within moments.

Epilogue
Three years later

৪০

Marla looked at her babies as they played joyously with their new puppy. She marveled that these triplets could be hers. Two boys and one girl, they were perfect in every way—and hell on her nerves at times. But it was all worth it.

Her children had Steele's eyes and her dark red hair. They were, in a word, beautiful.

Steele came to sit next to her, kissing her softly and taking her into his arms. "I've got to work tonight."

Marla had learned not to be completely terrified when Steele had to work. He was impervious to bullets—surely that was consolation enough to keep her from worrying. But it wasn't. She always worried about him. He was her husband, after all. Who else was entitled to worry over him?

"Come into the bedroom with me," he cajoled.

Marla shuddered with remembered ecstasy. Over the years their sex had become more explosive, never waning, always savagely hot and amazing. "I can't. The babies can't be left alone."

"That's why Deirdre is coming to pick them up any minute."

Right on cue there came a knock at the door. Deirdre came in, all smiles and sunshine, for everyone doted on the triplets. She gathered the children and the puppy to take them back to her own apartment within the Sterling compound.

The minute the door closed behind Deirdre, Steele was upon her like a ravenous beast. He kissed her long and deep, his tongue dueling with hers, filling her with his unique flavor. He tore her clothes from her with impatient hands and had them both nude within seconds.

He thrust two fingers into her wet heat and suckled a breast fully into his mouth, tonguing the nipple to stabbing hardness in his hot, moist mouth. Marla wrapped her legs around his waist and held on for dear life. His head moved up her breasts to her chest and throat and at long last her mouth. He kissed her as if he'd never stop kissing her again. As if it was the first or last time for both of them.

He spread her legs wide for him and came down between them, thrusting his turgid length deep into the wet heat of her pleasure hole. Marla gasped and wrapped her legs around his waist, bringing him even deeper into her body. Steele's hands came up to play with her nipples, pinching and stroking them to diamond hardness.

He held her breasts still as he rocked upon her, filling her up over and over again with the thick, heavy weight of his penis. Marla let her fingers roam down over her pussy, zeroing in on her clit. She rubbed there, mindless in her passion, breathless with anticipation. Steele thrust hard, savagely into her. Marla cried out. Steele groaned. The lights flickered even though Marla wore her grounding bracelet.

They came together, moaning and gasping, holding each other tight.

Marla knew she was pregnant again. She could already instinctively, impossibly feel it.

"I love you, Steele," she breathed.

"I love you too, Marla. I'll love you forever."

The lights flickered then went out, cocooning them in darkness.

Vicious

ᏝᎧ

Trademarks Acknowledgement

~

Prologue

ℬ

John Spada fell back against the wall of what looked to be an abandoned warehouse, the taste of copper heavy on his tongue from where he'd bitten it. How he'd gotten here he didn't know. He had no recollection of ever leaving his bedroom since going to bed for the night.

He looked down at the sticky red stains on his hands. Blood. But from where? He felt himself, checking for wounds and realizing with dread that the question wasn't *where* the blood was from, but *who*. It certainly wasn't his.

John looked down at his attire, all black—from his tight-fitting T-shirt, jeans and boots to a long, flaring trench coat. He was also wearing a wide-brimmed bootlegger's hat—the kind a bootlegging rogue would have worn, at a rakish angle, during the height of prohibition. He recognized the hat as his grandfather's, and his coat as one he'd just recently bought, but he'd never seen the other clothes before and he had no idea how he'd come to be wearing them. They felt new. He reached into the pocket of his trench coat and found nothing but a small stack of business cards.

Johnny Vicious
Vigilante

That was all they read, in bolded copperplate, short and simple. But John had no idea who this Johnny Vicious was or why he should have so many of his business cards in his pocket.

Looking around, he came to recognize the surrounding architecture. He was in downtown Cleveland, just thirty minutes from his home in Akron. But how on earth had he gotten here? He glanced about wildly, hoping to see his car parked nearby, when the shouts reached his ears.

He dared a look around the corner of the building and saw a small group of surly-looking thugs. They caught sight of him and began running toward him full tilt. One of them pulled a gun and fired, the bullet glancing off the concrete façade of the building so that shards of the stone hit John, scraping his cheek and drawing blood.

Without thinking he reached beneath his trench coat to the two enormous guns holstered, side by side, at the back waistband of his black slacks and drew them. He'd never seen the guns before, had no idea why he had them. He was a cop, his standard-issue Beretta more than enough firepower for him. So far as he knew, he owned no other guns.

The three thugs rounded the corner and the one holding the gun fired again.

A blind rush of adrenaline surged through him and time seemed to slow. Seconds became minutes, became hours. John could see the bullet floating through the air toward him straight from the barrel of the thug's handgun. He stepped out of the way of the bullet, as easily as if he were simply dodging someone on the street. The bullet whizzed past him and time resumed its normal flow again, stunning him.

"Stop, I'm with the police," he shouted, even as he felt his fingers tighten on the triggers of the guns.

The thugs ignored him and advanced. The gunman took a chance and rushed him. John's fingers shook upon the trigger, the guns wobbled. Then a sort of steel crept up his spine. He gritted his jaw and yelled a warning even as he instinctively fired one of his guns.

He struck the gun-toting thug in the wrist with a loud explosion from his hand cannon. The thug screamed and clutched his shredded, bloodied hand to his chest, dropping his gun uselessly to the ground. The other two took one look at the size of John's guns, shared a look between each other and fled, practically dragging their wounded friend in their wake.

John looked at the guns in his hands as if they were monsters. But he couldn't resist the impulse to holster them once more at his back with deft familiarity.

What was going on?

The world abruptly grayed out and John Spada knew no more.

Chapter One
One year later

୨୦

Enya's bare feet slapped hard against the wet pavement as she fled down the cramped alleyway nestled between her apartment building and the one next to it. She dared a look back and her heart quailed as she saw the two great hulking men still in hot pursuit.

She ran faster, until her heart pumped fire and her lungs breathed smoke. But the hit men were still dogging her every step. She veered sharply to the right and ran down yet another alleyway, this time wildly searching for a place to hide. There was none. The alley ended at a fence, effectively penning her in. She was trapped with no place to go.

Enya shivered in the cool, drizzling rain. She was wearing only the T-shirt and shorts she normally slept in. She didn't want to die in her pajamas. With fierce determination she put one foot upon the fence and began scaling it. Her tender feet screamed at the abuse, but Enya was oblivious to the pain, so intent was she to escape.

"There she is," she heard one of her pursuers shout, and she looked back to see them rounding the corner and closing in on her fast. She quickened her pace and made her way over the fence in record time. Her feet slapped painfully against the ground as she jumped down and turned to run.

She smacked into the chest of a man standing directly behind her, so hard that it nearly knocked her down.

The man's hands shot out and kept her from falling.

"Are you all right?" he asked in a dark, smoky voice.

Enya tried to see his face beneath his wide-brimmed hat, but the shadows hid every nuance of it. "Those men are after me," she said in a rush, pointing back across the fence. "We have to go, now!"

"There's no need to run," he said calmly.

"They're going to kill me, and you too if they see you with me," she panted.

"Don't be afraid."

The man put her behind him as one of her pursuers dropped down from the fence. The man's long, black coat flared out behind him, tickling her cold legs with a strange sort of warmth. "Stay back," he told her over his shoulder.

"Who the fuck are you?" demanded the hit man.

"I'm Johnny Vicious. And you were just leaving."

Enya's heart beat a wild pulse in her chest.

The hit man laughed and drew a gun. "I don't think you're in any position to be telling me when to leave."

He fired the gun and something miraculous happened.

Johnny pushed her to the side and his body seemed to grow hazy, faint. One blink and she would have missed it. He was moving so fast he was little more than an indistinct blur for her eyes to trip over.

The hit man grunted when something struck his hand, sending his gun flying. It skidded against the wet ground and landed at Enya's feet. She picked up the weapon and held fast to it in case she found a need to use it. Not that she'd ever used a gun before—she just hoped to point and shoot and hit something, anything, if it came down to it.

Johnny reappeared behind the man and kicked him brutally in the kidneys so that he fell, gasping, to the ground. Just then, the second hit man dropped from the fence to the ground and fired his gun at Johnny, point blank.

Somehow Johnny moved out of the line of fire, his motions so fast that Enya could barely follow them with her eyes. It looked as if he disappeared completely for a moment then reappeared once more, safely out of the path of the bullet. He leaned back as a second bullet whizzed past him. The hit man fired again, and again Johnny dodged the bullets with lightning swift, graceful movements that looked like magic, moving so fast that he appeared to disappear and reappear at will.

Johnny struck out for the man's face, crushing his nose in a spray of blood. The man screamed in rage and pain and fired his gun several times in succession. Johnny seemed to disappear again and when he reappeared he had the man in a headlock, suppressing his air. The man passed out almost immediately, falling limp to the ground right next to his comrade, who was still dazed with his own pain.

Enya's eyes were wide as Johnny turned and looked at her. He seemed to blur again and one second later he'd wrested the gun from her hands. She hadn't been able to stop him from doing it.

"You should go back home, pretty eyes," he told her, removing the clip and tossing the gun to the ground. "I'll take care of these two."

"If I go home they'll just send more after me," she said shakily, knowing it was true.

"I'll make sure the proper authorities know about this. You'll be safe enough. Trust me. You can go home." A tiny shaft of light fell over the corner of Johnny's mouth as he smiled. He moved even closer to her and waved his hands before her face. A tiny flick of his wrist and a card appeared. He traced one corner of it down the side of her cheek, a sensuous whisper of a touch that made her catch her breath. He stepped back and held out the card, waiting for her to take it.

"Go home now," he told her sternly, his smile disappearing completely.

Enya clutched the card tight in her hand, turned and ran down the alleyway in search of home, never once looking back.

Chapter Two
Later that night

෨

"So the FBI will have a guard outside your door day and night, and we'll have a black and white parked outside at all times. You'll be safe enough here."

Enya gritted her teeth, shaking her head at the detective speaking to her. She hated having her privacy invaded like this. But what else could she do? Johnny Vicious had called the cops for her, anonymously of course, and they in turn had called the federal agents who were assigned to her case. She had no choice but to put up with being placed under a microscope.

"Ms. Merritt, we're doing all we can to ensure that this doesn't happen again," the detective said defensively.

Enya forced a smile. "I know, and I thank you. Really. I do. It's just a lot to get used to all at once."

The detective smiled at her. "I understand how you feel."

Enya moved past him and waded through the uniformed officers as they gathered what evidence they could. She went to her bedroom to find it full of yet more officers. With a wince, she turned toward her bathroom.

Empty. Finally some peace and quiet.

She sat on the toilet, placed her elbows on her knees and rested her head wearily in her hands. She hated this. She was a solitary computer geek. A code monkey. She didn't have the patience for all these strangers in and about her home. Enya found it very nearly horrific to imagine who the coming days might bring to her doorstep.

A shower. She needed a shower. A nice long soak under the hot spray would help acclimate her to her new environment.

She pulled up her T-shirt, exposing her breasts to the cooler air. Enya let the shirt fall to the floor. Her nipples stabbed hard into the air, long and tight on the crest of her large, round breasts. She looked down at her dusky, cinnamon skin—a gift from her Arabian ancestors—and decided she needed to lose a good twenty pounds.

A noise just outside the door made her jump. Her eyes flew to the handle of the door—which was unlocked! She made a wild dash and locked it just as the handle began to turn from the other side. Enya heaved a huge sigh of relief and leaned against the door. Then she went about removing the rest of her clothes.

The water splashed on her head with all the force of a raging storm. She adjusted the spray, setting it to massaging pulses with the turn of a dial, and lathered her long, black hair.

Several long, luxurious minutes later, Enya was lulled into daydreams when the image of Johnny Vicious flashed bright in her mind.

All she'd seen of him was his mouth, but oh how luscious it had been. Just full enough to be suckable, just hard enough to be completely male. His body had been a dark blur in the night, but her imagination filled in all the blanks left by that billowing trench coat of his.

He was at least a head taller than her, even without the bootlegger's hat. His legs were long and lean through the calf, but thicker in the thighs. Much thicker. His chest was wide, as were his shoulders. And his hair would be a delicious chocolate brown. Glossy and sleek in the night, just like everything else about him.

Enya again replayed the moment when he'd traced the corner of his calling card down her cheek. She felt a wild despair and very nearly panted with a rush of desire. Who had he been, this Johnny Vicious? A good Samaritan? Not bloody likely with that blurring trick of his. Who then?

She couldn't begin to guess.

But oh how she wished she knew.

Had his arm brushed her breast when he'd swept her behind him? She burned with the memory, for he *had* brushed her. He'd faced her foes like a hero, but he had handled her like a roué. He'd nearly picked her up with but the strength of his arm.

Enya couldn't ever remember being this horny. And over a man whose face she barely knew? It boggled the mind. It boggled *her* mind. She rubbed her hands over her stabbing nipples and had to bite back a groan. She didn't think she'd felt this hot in a very long time.

She let one of her hands twist a long, aching nipple while the other trailed down to play with the lips of her sex. She was syrupy slick with her juices and the water, so her fingers were slippery against her. She allowed her fingertips to barely brush over her clit and felt her knees melt.

Freeing her nipple, she reached overhead and took down the showerhead. Its heavy pulses of water washed down over her, sluices of it caressing every inch of her skin. She adjusted the spray, held the head cupped in her hand and positioned it against her pussy.

She imagined the pulses of water were Johnny Vicious' fingers.

With one hand she held the showerhead while the other parted the lips of her cunt, opening herself to the spray of water. She separated her middle finger from the others and slid it deep into her pussy, moaning a heavy sigh into the gathered steam of the shower.

The water caressed her clit, pummeling it with bursts of fluid until it was heavy and tingling. Her finger crooked and thrust in and out of her body. Her hips beat out a steady, bucking rhythm against her hand.

And she nearly swooned with her climax. Her body shuddered and an unbelievable release of tension had her sinking to her knees in the stall.

Several long, blissful moments later, she turned off the water and stepped into a thick, plush terry cloth robe hanging from a hook on the door. She put Johnny's card, already becoming dog-eared, in the pocket over her left breast. She realized with some small surprise that she hadn't told anyone about Johnny Vicious yet.

It was going on three in the morning, and her police protection changed shifts precisely at three-fifteen. Enya supposed the black and white car would pull away while a second one took its place. She looked out the window, down at the street where the present patrol car waited. She watched it pull away and waited to see the other one come up. She was surprised by the ringing of her doorbell.

She answered it, fully expecting it to be her FBI bodyguard, Agent Danvers. It was.

"Can I come in, Ms. Merritt?" he asked.

Enya frowned at his seeming hesitancy in asking her. "Sure. Of course." She opened the door wider for him and tried not to let him brush her body as he passed.

"I suppose you're really scared now," he said after clearing his throat awkwardly.

Enya smiled. "Not with you here. And my police guard too," she said, pointing toward the window.

"Is there a guard down there now?" the agent asked.

Enya glanced out the window again and found no trace of another car yet.

"No," she said, and was taken completely off guard when she turned back around to find the agent right behind her.

He flicked open the curtains, looked out and nodded to himself.

"Well," Agent Danvers sighed heavily. "You really should be afraid, you know. Very afraid."

Enya felt a cold wash of fear spill down her spine as he turned to her with menace in his eyes.

Chapter Three

෨

Enya dashed for the door. The agent caught up to her, wrapped his arm around her throat and slung her around. She fell to the floor and thumped her head against it, hard. Shocked and dazed, she gathered her breath to scream, but the man placed his hand over her mouth before she could utter a sound.

She wriggled and squirmed, trying to break free, but the man straddled her, his hand remaining a bruising pressure against her lips, trapping her most effectively.

A bright silver flash glinted off the edge of his knife. He gently trailed it against her cheek, just as Johnny Vicious had done with his card earlier. But where earlier such a caress had seduced her, now it only sickened her.

"We're going to have a talk, you and I. You're going to tell me everything you've told the feds about Siren. You're going to tell me about every scrap of evidence you've given them. And I'm going to tell you how we deal with traitors like you in this big business world."

He eased his hand back and Enya struck, clamping her teeth down on his fingers, drawing blood. He cried out and jerked his hand away, falling back and affording her the opportunity to wriggle away. She gained her knees and scurried toward the window overlooking the street. She didn't make it before the agent's hand wrapped around her ankle and pulled her sharply back.

Her fingers caught in the lace of her curtain as he dragged her down, and the window treatment fell away, catching and tangling on top of their struggling forms.

He straddled her again, slapping the side of her face so hard that stars swam before her eyes. When her vision cleared she glared up at her attacker. The only defensive weapon she had left was her pride.

"Tell me everything. You *will* tell me everything or I swear I'll cut your throat. Do you hear me?" he panted down into her face.

Enya gathered spit in her mouth and sprayed it at him. "Fuck you. Don't you think they'll know who did this? Don't you think they'll hunt you down like a dog? I'm a star witness and your FBI buddies have been planning this coup for almost a decade. They want to see Siren go down almost as much as I do for the things they've done! No way am I letting a little mole like you know what I've said. Or what I've still got left to say!"

He slapped her and she tasted blood in her mouth again. Hers.

Suddenly her front door opened with a crunch of wood and a crash of noise. An officer in a black uniform rushed into the room, taking the scene in immediately. He pulled her assailant from her and hit him over the head with his baton. The rogue FBI agent fell unconscious to the floor at his feet.

"Oh my God, how did you know?" Enya panted, crawling away from the fallen form of her enemy.

"I saw your curtains fall from below." He helped her up with a strong, steady hand. "Are you all right?"

"Why were you late?" She glared at him, going from frightened to angry in less than two seconds.

"I wasn't late. My predecessor was in a hurry to get home and left a couple of minutes early. An action that will never happen again, believe me."

"A couple of minutes were all it took to nearly kill me," she gritted out, rubbing at the hard knot that was already forming at the back of her head.

"I'm John Spada. I'm going to take care of you, don't worry," he said. A small, smug smile twisted his lips as he bent down and handcuffed her still unconscious assailant.

A stroke of memory teased at her mind, then was gone.

He walked her through the ruin that had been her front door and led her to the elevator. They were silent within it, but it was almost a comfortable silence, as if both were used to this sort of thing. Enya realized she was barefoot and still wearing nothing but her robe, and nearly laughed.

She was going into shock. Even she knew that.

Being attacked twice in one night could be taxing on a girl.

John Spada led her to his car, his hand tight upon her elbow, guiding her lest she stumble or fall behind. He opened the passenger door for her and Enya gave a silent moment of thanks that he didn't make her sit in the backseat, behind the cage. She didn't think she could have handled that tonight.

Enya rested in the confines of the patrol car, and in the few seconds it took him to walk around and get in on the driver's side, she had already infused her lungs with the scent of him. It was prevalent in the very fibers of the car, enveloping her in a delicious, woodsy scent that calmed her even more than her steamy shower had.

John pulled the car onto the street and drove slowly down the road. He pressed a button on the walkie-talkie fastened at his shoulder.

"Dispatch, patch me through to the chief."

A minute passed in silence. Then, "Chief, this is Spada. I'm with Enya Merritt now. She was attacked by Agent Danvers. My guess is he's on Siren's payroll. I left him cuffed in Enya's apartment."

He listened for a moment then let go of the walkie-talkie.

"We're going to the station," he said.

"I don't want to go to the station," she said in a rush. "Who knows how many more want me killed? If Siren is big enough to get the FBI on their payroll, I don't think a few cops are going to be able to stand in their way."

"They don't have the whole FBI, just one rogue agent."

"There could be others. Damn it, this is just the sort of thing I wanted to avoid when I started this."

"What do you know that has them wanting you dead?"

"I worked for them. I found out some nasty things about them while I did. So I'm blowing the whistle on their embezzling and money laundering. They've lied, cheated and stolen to get to the top. Genetic testing, chemical warfare, blood money—you name it and they've got their finger in the pie. And it goes all the way to the top of the company."

"We'll go to the station and see if we can't move you to another location. After that I promise to stay near you, to make sure this doesn't happen again." John maneuvered the car through downtown Cleveland's light, early morning traffic with the ease of a pro.

"I don't need a babysitter. I need a time machine. I want to go back to the moment when I called the FBI and stop myself from doing it."

"Don't say that. Don't ever say that. Justice will be served to these bastards at Siren. Have a little faith in the system."

"My faith has been used up for the night," she said wearily.

* * * * *

Seven hours later

"We've prepared a safe haven for you. A quiet cabin outside of the city. Only myself and Officer Spada will know where you are."

Enya eyed the chief of police warily. "Can't I get a detective to help guard me? I mean, a street cop might not—"

"John Spada is only a street cop because he still chooses to be. He's one of my best men. He'll take good care of you."

Enya subsided. "How long will I have to stay at this cabin of yours?"

The chief sighed. "Quite frankly, I don't know. Maybe a few days. Maybe a week. I just don't know."

"My life wasn't supposed to be interrupted like this. The FBI promised me that I would be safe."

"The FBI is busy taking care of their mole. When they're sure no one else in their ranks is with Siren, they'll take over your case again. Until then, I'm responsible for your safety. And I do mean to keep you safe. Now Spada is waiting for you just outside the door. Go."

Enya had a thousand things she wanted to say, but she took one look at the chief's stern face and held her tongue.

She hadn't slept in almost twenty-four hours. She was tired and aching from her tussle with Agent Danvers, and irritable because of it. She only hoped Spada didn't mind her passing out in her seat on the way out of the city. At least someone had brought her some clothes and shoes from her apartment. Enya didn't think she could handle being half naked right now along with everything else.

To top things off, her bruised and bloodied feet were still stinging something fierce, even in her soft, worn sneakers.

She left the room, which had been her haven for all of seven hours, and bumped into Spada with a jolt.

Another bit of memory stirred in her mind and then was gone.

"Chief says you're to come with me," he said gently. His light green eyes roved over her from head to toe, as if he was determined that no part of her would be harmed during his watch. Enya was grateful for that much at least.

She reached into her pocket and fingered the card there, finding some small measure of courage in doing so.

Spada's hand was warm on the small of her back as he guided her through the bustling office full of uniformed and plain-clothed police officers. Once in the car, she relaxed somewhat and felt the stressful, horrific events of the past day finally overcome her. She cried in silence. Taking the handkerchief Spada gently offered, she blotted her tears away until they were done flowing.

"I'm sorry," she said at last.

"I'd be worried if you didn't cry," he said quietly. "It's a lot to take in, having one's life turned upside down like this. You're bound to feel the stress sooner or later."

"It *is* a lot to take in," she agreed, and fell silent. She reached into her pocket again and this time took out the card. Just looking at it made her feel worlds better.

"Have you ever heard of Johnny Vicious?" she asked him.

His hands jerked so hard on the wheel that the car swerved, but he recovered control quickly.

"I can see that you have," she said drolly.

"Where do you know that name from?" he asked, voice hard.

"Nowhere," she lied. "I found this business card with his name on it and it intrigued me."

"Let me see it," he growled.

"No," she held tight to it.

"Give it to me, Enya," he demanded. He pulled the car over to the side of the road and slammed on the brakes. "*Now*."

Enya handed it over to him reluctantly. He took one look at it and rolled down his window. Enya saw what he meant to do and cried out a protest. He threw it out the window and pulled the car back onto the road, picking up speed.

"You asshole," she said. "That was *mine*."

"You have no business keeping something like that a secret from me."

"What are you talking about? It's no secret. I just found the thing—"

"You didn't just find it," he snorted.

"So," she countered, "what do you know about Vicious— this so-called vigilante—that has you so uptight?"

"My colleagues and I have heard of Vicious' exploits far and wide. It's only a matter of time before he's caught. I know he's bad news and you should stay away from him."

"I'll be the judge of that," she said stiffly. "He saved my life you know."

"Did you see his face?" he asked, suddenly intent on her answer. "No one has ever seen his face."

"I saw his lips." She nearly sighed with the memory of it.

"I don't suppose you can positively I.D. a person just by looking at their lips," he said drolly.

"Maybe I could. They were very memorable lips." She smiled.

"Oh God, you're taken with him," he said, aghast.

"No I'm not," she lied. Spada gave her a hard look and she chuckled. "Okay, so maybe just a little. But you would be too if you could just see him in action. He's like some kind of magician with the way he moves. It's amazing."

"I've heard all this before," he said. "Every time he saves someone, he leaves them wanting more. Men *and* women. It's pathetic."

"I think he's wildly romantic."

"Oh God, give me a break," he groaned.

"Well he is. A vigilante out saving lives, what's not to like about that?"

"He's taking the law into his own hands. That's completely illegal," he said sternly.

"So? He helps people."

"Breaking the law never helped anybody."

"I'd be dead now if it weren't for him," she growled. "Those thugs who chased me last night, they were going to shoot me. Vicious saved me from them. And it was amazing to watch him do it."

"He moves like lightning, so I've heard," Spada said softly.

"He does. It's the most incredible thing I've ever seen. He actually dodged bullets! And I bet if he wanted to he could walk between raindrops. If you could just see him you'd realize how cool he is."

"If I could see him, I'd cuff him and lock him up."

"Oh please," she snorted. "You can't be that white bread."

"Oh, but I can—" He broke off with a savage curse as a truck slammed into the back of his car.

Enya screamed as the car swerved off the road going sixty miles an hour. The truck sped up and hit them again, this time tipping the car into a full spin. Spada got the car back under his control with firm, strong hands and sped up, leaving the truck behind.

"Dispatch, this is Spada. We're under attack, repeat, under attack! Request backup immediately," Spada quickly rattled off into his walkie-talkie.

"Where are you, Spada, over?" came the tinny voice from the small speaker on the walkie-talkie.

Spada gritted his teeth and glanced at Enya. "If I tell Dispatch where we are they're sure to know where we're headed. The safe house isn't far from here."

"Then can we outrun these guys?" she asked, looking out the back window at the truck still hounding after them.

"Hold on and we'll find out," Spada said, and put the pedal to the metal.

The patrol car's engine roared and they sped up to a hundred and ten miles per hour. The truck sank behind them as they pulled away.

"They must have been waiting at the station and followed us out here," Spada growled.

"We're pulling away from them," she said, still watching out the back. "Hurry."

"I *am* hurrying."

"Well hurry *more*," Enya demanded.

The car sped up a little more as Spada pushed its limits. The truck sank back down over the horizon, losing ground, unable to catch up.

"I think we're okay," she said after a few minutes of watching. "God," she exclaimed, "what the hell was that all about?"

"They must really want you bad to try a stunt like that. But I promised to keep you safe, and keep you safe I will. We're almost to the house now."

They pulled off onto a small, gravel road, which meandered into the woods, away from the highway. They drove on in silence for several long minutes as the miles passed. The road wound in sharp curves, deeper and deeper into the woods until they pulled up to a small wooden cabin nestled among the trees.

"Home sweet home, at least for a little while," Spada drawled. He got out and retrieved her overnight bag full of clothes from the backseat and his large, silver briefcase. "I'll call the chief and let him know what happened."

Enya looked at the tiny, quaint cabin and sighed. "Well, here we go. Let's see how long this lasts."

Chapter Four
Two days later

John Spada looked down at Enya as she slept in the bed. Her black hair was spread out on the pillow, lending her a wanton, wild look in her soft cotton pajamas. Her face was full of character. Black flaring eyebrows over her closed brown eyes, straight little nose and full, rosy lips. She only stood to his shoulder, she was so petite. But she wasn't slender — she was full and rounded and completely feminine. She was quite lovely. He'd noticed that right away.

But how resilient she would prove to be in the coming days was still in question. He could easily tell that she was already becoming quite bored, cooped up as she was. It couldn't be helped. He was determined to keep her safe, and that meant staying put.

Siren was sticking their necks out on the chopping block, having tried three times to kill her. John knew there was a price on her head. A million dollars to the man who shut her up was a hefty bounty, but Siren could more than afford it.

The FBI was determined to take Siren down. The huge conglomerate had bucked in the face of the law one too many times, and now they'd been caught red-handed by one of their own workers. They'd gotten sloppy. No amount of money was going to save them now.

But they wanted Enya dead anyway. For revenge, no doubt. To punish her for speaking out and doing the right thing. Sooner or later, if the FBI didn't get their act together, someone would succeed in taking her out.

John knew he wouldn't be allowed to stay by her side twenty-four-seven like this when they went back to the city. But he was determined, nevertheless, to keep her safe, even if he had to break a few rules while doing so.

Enya was likable on a level he'd never experienced with a woman. She was intelligent, witty and at times completely adorable. He knew she resented having him dog her every step, but he also knew she was trying to make his job a little easier too. She never wandered far when she went outside and spent most of her time just roaming about the cabin, cleaning this or that, watching television and reading.

She was an easy charge to guard.

He looked at her small, slender hand as it rested on the pillow by her head and realized he'd spent far too much time ogling her. What would she think if she woke up? She wouldn't like knowing that he checked on her once every hour of every night just to assure himself that she was still there. He left the room and went back into the kitchen to find a snack.

There wasn't much in the way of groceries. Suddenly that fact bothered him. He knew full well that he should stay and protect his charge, but the cabin seemed to have shrunk on him in the last half hour. He gave it a few moments' thought and finally let out a huge, frustrated sigh. Surely Enya would be safe if he stepped out. It was close to midnight, after all. She couldn't possibly get into any trouble at this hour, could she? He decided that he had to leave—if only for a few minutes—for his own sanity. And getting groceries at the nearest twenty-four-hour supermarket was as good a reason as any to do so. He grabbed his car keys and left the cabin quietly, careful not to make a noise that might wake Enya.

He got behind the wheel and started down the long driveway. He was heading for the highway when everything grayed out.

* * * * *

The cabin was small and lightly furnished. There was only one bedroom and one bed—which John insisted Enya take—so

John had been spending his nights on the sofa. The wooded surroundings lent a privacy that Enya had never really experienced before, being used to the sounds of the city around her at all times. The sound of the crickets at night was deafening.

The kitchen was small, with a tiny breakfast table in the middle. There hadn't been many groceries, just the staples of bread, milk, cheese…those sorts of things. They'd been subsisting off grilled cheese sandwiches and tomato soup for the most part. In many ways it felt a lot like camping.

During the days Enya tried watching soap operas on the television set, but she'd had no luck in following the storylines. Soaps were just too complicated, too demanding of large amounts of time for her liking. She tried reading one of the books on the bookshelves, but her mind had refused to focus long enough for her to become engrossed in the plot.

Out of boredom, Enya had trekked through the woods around the house. John had hung back politely, determined to stay near and never lose sight of her.

She'd never seen so many trees. There was a small babbling brook not a hundred feet from the cabin, and Enya had taken her shoes off to walk in it and enjoy the feeling of being closer to nature than she ever had before.

John was there with her every minute of the day, watching over her like a hawk. At first it had bothered her greatly—John didn't even let her out the front door without being at her side—but she'd quickly grown accustomed to having him near. She had no choice, really.

Being cooped up with John Spada proved to be much more fun than Enya would have guessed. He was witty and charming and considerate. Not to mention he was very easy on the eyes. He saw to her every need and was gentle in handling her. Enya hadn't felt so safe since the whole fiasco started.

Which is why she panicked when, just after midnight, she woke up to find him gone. His briefcase, even his car, was gone. Just gone. With no word and no warning.

There was no phone for her to call the station and ask where Spada might be. There was no way for her to contact him directly. She was stuck out in the middle of nowhere, hunted, afraid and completely alone.

She searched the house and the yard surrounding it. Calling out John's name over and over again, getting no response to her cries. There was no note, nothing to prove he was coming back anytime soon. Enya grabbed a bottle of water from the fridge and went back to her room, trying to ignore the feeling of foreboding that plagued her.

What she found there stunned her.

"Hello again," Johnny Vicious said from the shadows, his lit cigarette a small dot of light in the blackness. His voice was dark and smoky, completely masculine.

"How did you find me?" she asked, her eyes adjusting to the darkness, startled to her toes to see him sitting in the rocking chair by the bed.

"I have my ways," he said, a smile in his voice. He stubbed his cigarette out on the heel of his boot. The wide brim of his hat, just visible in the darkness, hid his face, giving him an air of mystique that was impossible to ignore.

"What are you doing here?"

"Checking to be sure that you are safe," he said softly. "I've been thinking about you since that night. I wanted…I needed to know that you were safe."

"I don't know *how* safe I am. Officer Spada left without a word."

"I know. I'm sure he didn't mean to frighten you. He probably didn't think you'd wake up while he was out."

"Maybe he was in a hurry. It just doesn't seem like him to abandon his post, that's all."

"Oh, John Spada is very steadfast when it comes to his responsibilities."

Enya frowned. "You know John?"

"We're acquainted, though I believe he doesn't know it yet," he said cryptically.

"Maybe he's in denial," she offered, smiling

"You have no idea," he drawled.

Her smile disappeared. "Who *are* you, Johnny Vicious?"

"I'm nobody. I am vapor. A memory only. No one knows me, so I barely exist."

"It must be lonely," she said softly.

"It wasn't…until the other night when I watched you go."

As romantic words went, those melted her knees like butter.

"Can I turn on the light?" she asked shakily.

"No," he said in a hard voice that would have sent chills down her spine if she didn't know he was here to seduce her. "Leave the light off. I like the mystery of it."

"I'm not going to sleep with a man whose face I don't know," she gritted out.

Johnny laughed. "What makes you think I want to sleep with you? I assure you that sleep is the furthest thing from my mind."

"Funny. But I'll have to ask you to leave all the same. I'm not in the market for a one-night stand. I've got enough on my plate without the complication, thank you."

"A kiss, then. Just grant me one kiss and I'll leave."

Enya felt her heart skip a beat. She closed the gap between them in silence. Even sitting, his head was even with hers. She felt his breath on her face, sweet and warm, like a ray of sunshine, and sighed with bliss.

"One kiss." She bent her face to him, pushing his hat back a little to allow her access to his lips. Even with the hat pushed up, she couldn't see his face in the darkness. She closed her eyes and let the moment take her.

His mouth was like silken fire against hers. He tasted like clove cigarettes and spicy masculinity. He smelled like the rain and the wind on a blustery day. She folded into his arms, seeking a closer warmth.

One minute she was in charge, initiating the kiss, the next he had her in his lap, arms tight around her. His mouth slanted over hers, his tongue slipping between her lips to play against her own. His flavor blossomed in her mouth, like a flower opening to the sun.

His lips hardened on hers, taking now instead of giving, and she gasped, giving way to his rapacious kiss. He caught her breath and gave his back to her, infusing her with the very essence of his life. Her body grew heavy with desire, and from the feel of his hard cock against her bottom, she knew he was feeling much the same as she. The fiery slide of his tongue on hers made her weak with wanting.

She moved against his erection and was pleased to hear his breath catch raggedly. She let her hands rove over him, from his incredibly wide shoulders to his waist, petting him. He was solidly built, all muscle and lean, hard man.

Abruptly he pulled back from her and set her back on her feet.

"I should go. I've taken too long as it is."

"Where will you go?" she asked.

His finger caressed her cheek. "I'll be close. Don't worry."

With that, he was gone, like a flicker of lightning that left no trace of him ever being in the room.

Chapter Five

∞

Johnny Vicious, AKA John Spada, knocked on the door to Ryan Murdock's office. He opened the door and stuck his head in the room. "Have you got a minute?"

"For you, Vicious, always. Have a seat." He motioned to a chair opposite his at the desk. "You've been absent the past few nights."

"John has been very busy," he said with a rakish smile. "I haven't had a moment to myself in over forty-eight hours."

Ryan Murdock refused to be intimidated by the very obviously dangerous man across from him. "You need to call us when you're going to be absent."

"In case you haven't noticed, I'm not able to just wrest control away from him like that." He snapped his fingers. "Danger or impatience is about the time I come in, and John's been lying low recently."

"He has a woman," Ryan stated emphatically.

Vicious tried and failed to contain his start of surprise. "You guys work fast," he drawled. "I'm very impressed."

"We make it a point to keep tabs on all our so-called 'vigilantes'. And Johnny, I'd really appreciate it if you stopped giving out business cards. We don't want to attract any undue attention, now would we?"

"But it's so romantic, don't you think?"

"What we're doing has nothing to do with romance." Ryan sighed. "Just say you'll try to call us when you're not checking in for the night, and that you'll retire the business card thing. Go on, even if you don't mean it. Just say it."

Johnny grinned, looking an awful lot like a shark. "I don't like to lie," he tsked.

"Please Vicious, I'm asking you as nicely as I can here."

"Oh all right. Since it's so important to you. I will try to call and phase out my calling card...thing."

"Good," Ryan said with some relief. "Now what did you want to see me about?"

"Don't you already know?" Vicious teased.

Ryan smiled.

"No way," Vicious said.

"Go ahead and pitch me the idea anyway, just so we're on the same page."

Vicious nodded his approval. "I want Enya. So does John. I want her to come here, under your protection, while this business with Siren blows over."

"Siren is determined to kill her," Ryan said plainly.

"But Siren isn't a threat to you. And I know you'll take the best care of Enya. She'll be safe here."

"Have you asked her if that's what she wants?"

"I haven't really found the time, no," Vicious said with a wry chuckle. "But whether she wants to or not, I'll have her here within a few days. Count on it. You can take care of the FBI. Promise to cooperate, bribe 'em or whatever it takes to get them to back off so she can stay here. I know you can do this."

"You seem to think we have an awful lot of power over the law."

"Don't you?" Vicious tossed back.

It was Ryan Murdock's turn to wear a rakish grin. "We might."

"Well then, how about it?" Vicious pressed.

"How will Spada feel about all this? Won't he want to know why we're suddenly taking over the case?"

"I don't care. He'll see that she's safe here. He must. Don't worry about it."

"Are you trying to convince me or yourself?" Ryan asked knowingly.

"Good question," Vicious admitted. "You know what? I don't know the answer to that one myself."

"Well you'd better find out quick," Ryan said.

* * * * *

When Enya woke up the next morning, John Spada had returned. She caught him sleeping on the couch and took the moment to study him.

He was very tall, that much she already knew. But what she didn't know was that his face, in sleep, was almost too beautiful to be a man's. His skin was bronzed with the kiss of the sun, his chocolate brown hair infused with rich golden highlights. His lashes were long, like dark fans lying against his cheeks. His nose was straight and narrow, his jaw square and strong with a hint of five o'clock shadow.

His neck was thick with muscle that led down to his torso. He wasn't a large man, but he was very definitely well built. His hips were narrow, his legs long and muscled beneath his jeans, his thighs much thicker than his calves.

She didn't want to be attracted to him right now. Right now she was still mad at him for leaving her in the middle of the night.

She pulled a cushion from the couch and hit him on the head with it. He woke with a jolt, gaining his feet so fast it startled her.

A whisper of a memory teased at the back of her mind.

"Where were you last night?" she demanded.

He glared at her. "I went out to get us some more groceries. I don't know about you, but I'm tired of tomato soup and grilled cheese sandwiches."

"At midnight? You went out at midnight, with no word or warning, to get us groceries?" she asked, incredulous.

"I didn't think you'd get up while I was gone."

They glared at each other.

"Fine," Enya said at last. "Just don't ever leave like that again. I was scared out of my gourd when I found you'd gone."

"I'm sorry. Did anything eventful happen while I was gone?"

"No," she lied easily. "I just got up for some water and went back to bed. What else could I have done?"

He eyed her as if he didn't for one moment believe her. "You'd tell me if anything happened, wouldn't you?"

"Of course." She tried not to feel guilty that she was so blatantly lying to him, and failed.

John gave a heavy sigh and ran his hands through his hair. "Come on, how does Cap'n Crunch for breakfast sound?"

"It sounds great." She followed him into the kitchen to help prepare it.

Chapter Six

ຄວ

"Got any twos?"

"Go fish."

John took a card from the deck.

"Got any sevens?" Enya asked.

"Damn it. Here you go." He handed her a card.

"Is it just me or are we really bored?" she asked.

John laughed. "Cabin fever sucks."

"Let's watch some TV," she suggested, tossing her cards on the table.

They went into the small sitting room and turned the television on. It hummed to life, tuned to a news channel. What Enya heard made her heart thud a nervous rhythm and she sat down on the sofa next to John, hard.

The spokesman for Siren Corporation was unavailable for comment. But with two executives now under arrest for questionable research it's no wonder the conglomerate is keeping quiet. Federal officials have commandeered the main office of Siren here in Cleveland, and it's not clear yet if there'll be anymore arrests, though there is heavy speculation.

John flipped the channel and bright, cheery cartoons filled the silence between them.

"You're doing the right thing, you know," he said at length, gently.

"I thought I was, at first. But after all this, I almost wish I'd kept my mouth shut."

"Justice is never easy. I've been a cop for nine years and I often wonder if it's worth it. So many criminals slip through the cracks in the system, it's a wonder we have any in prisons."

"What will happen to me when this is all over? I don't even have a job anymore. And who would hire a narc like me now anyway? I certainly wouldn't."

"Not every business is as corrupt as Siren. You'll find work again," he said encouragingly.

"I wish I could be as confident as you sound," she said, watching the brightly colored cartoons on the screen.

"Everything will work out. You'll see."

"I just wish—" Her voice caught and she tried again. "I just wish that I hadn't been the one. That somebody else had discovered all this. That's what I wish."

"But this happened to you. You can't undo it now. And you're doing what's right. That makes you a very brave and honest person if you ask me. It's more than most people would do, believe me." John took her hand in his.

A flame of desire flared to life as he touched her and they both snatched their hands back guiltily. It seemed that an undercurrent swept beneath them now, and neither could ignore nor deny it.

Enya felt her nipples tighten with anticipation. She knew the desire was a by-product of being in such close proximity to some very yummy maleness for so long. But she didn't care. She reveled in it.

John's gaze met hers and he reclaimed her hand in his. He brought her hand up to his mouth and pressed a soft kiss against it. His warm breath rolled over her skin, giving her goose bumps. All the while his gaze held hers—his green eyes alight with an inner core of fire.

With a hunger that was startling in its intensity, Enya realized she wanted him.

Badly.

This wasn't just by-product. This was a very real and dangerous need.

He turned her hand over and pressed a kiss to her palm, lingering there so that Enya felt every nuance of his caress.

"We shouldn't do this," he murmured against her palm. "You're distressed."

"I know what I want," she said, melting into him. "And this situation I'm in has nothing to do with it." Her eyes ate up the sight of his thick, strong neck as he swallowed.

He kissed her wrist and her pulse beat a heavy staccato against his lips. One of his hands crept up and toyed with a lock of her long, black hair. His mouth worked its way up her arm and he was soon at the crook of her shoulder and neck. He buried his mouth against her, burning her up.

His glossy, chocolate-colored hair fascinated her. It had since the first moment she'd seen it. She was a sucker for brunettes. Always had been. Now she let her hands tangle in his hair, feeling the warm silken texture of it slip between her fingers like water. He growled against her throat and she let out a breathless moan.

Somehow one of his hands found its way under her shirt. He stroked the round fullness of her belly and she gasped.

"I won't stop to ask again, Enya," he whispered. "Are you sure you're ready for this?"

She couldn't find the words, but she quickly nodded her head yes, lest he pull back.

Her acquiescence unleashed something wild in him and he took her beneath him on the couch, laying his body on top of hers. His hands were suddenly everywhere, and her clothing practically fell away. The front clasp of her bra caught and then released beneath his deft fingers, and Enya caught her breath.

He palmed her breasts, her nipples stabbing into the center of his hot, deft hands. He kneaded her full, round flesh for a moment then allowed his fingers to pluck at her long, hard nipples. Enya couldn't hold back her moan and she arched up against his touch with feline grace.

John unfastened her jeans and jerked them down her legs, tossing them to the floor. He tore off his shirt, tossing it in the same direction as her pants. His big, wide chest was far more muscular than she had guessed. He had rock-hard pecs and a six-pack of abs.

Enya had never in her life fucked someone as well built as he was.

He dwarfed her there on the couch, his green eyes blazing a trail over all her exposed skin. He cupped her sex through her panties and she felt herself grow very damp against his hand.

"That's it. Wet your panties for me baby doll," he growled.

She melted into his touch and arched against his hand. He pressed harder against her, stroking her through the thin silk. He dipped his dark head and caught one of her nipples in his mouth.

Enya keened a wild cry and clutched his head to her breast. He rooted and suckled against her until her nipple ached. Then he moved to her other breast and gave that one the same attention as the first. He used his teeth against her and she shivered.

His fingers found their way into her panties and toyed with the clean-shaven lips of her pussy. "God, you're so wet," he groaned against her flesh and thrust two long, hard fingers into her cunt.

She bucked against him, wantonly riding his hand. His thumb rubbed against her clit each time he thrust into her, making her crazed with lust. Her hands found the fastening of his jeans and fumbled. They were shaking so badly she only had his zipper half down before he took over, pulling his hand away from her pussy so that she groaned with the loss.

He had his pants off in record time. He wore silk boxers that quickly fell away as well. And when she caught sight of the enormous girth of his cock she nearly fainted.

God, he was thicker than her wrist!

He was at least ten inches long. Smooth and dark, his cock was beautiful. He shaved — something Enya had never experienced with a man. His sac was heavy and full beneath his erection, lovely and round and delicious to look at.

But he was so *thick*. She didn't know if she could take that much all at once.

The mushroom head, dark and engorged with blood, wept a tear of need and Enya caught it on her finger. She licked it away and John's gaze burned as he watched her tongue dart out to catch his flavor.

He fell on her like a beast, bringing her legs up to hook around his hips. Without a warning to prepare her, he thrust into her body and she gave a shriek. God! He filled her so full she felt sure she would bust. His cock was so heavy, so long and wide that she thought for a moment she might faint from the shock.

His fingers roamed over her body and sought out her clit. He zeroed in on his target, rubbing and squeezing her until she was swollen and aching. He flicked her and she bucked against him, taking him deeper.

"Come on baby doll, you've still got a few inches to take," he growled.

She melted and felt her body take his. He sank in balls deep and groaned into her ear.

"God, you feel so fucking *good*," he said.

He pulled her legs up higher, sliding impossibly deeper into her body. He hooked her ankles behind his neck and began riding her. He slid in and out of her body as if he'd been made to fit there. Enya couldn't believe it but she felt the first pulses of her climax and cried out.

John rubbed her clit until she milked him with her release. She came so hard she saw stars, and when she came back to herself it was to find John's gaze waiting to catch with hers.

"I'm not done with you yet," he murmured and thrust into her, hard, stretching her to fit him.

They looked into each other's eyes for long, delicious minutes during which he thrust in and out of her countless times. He reached into the center of her and touched her heart. Her pulse beat at the back of her throat and she clutched her legs tighter about his neck.

He brought his hands around, squeezing her bottom, lifting her even higher against him. He traced the seam of her ass, tickling her. Seducing her into another release, he thrust harder and toyed with her clit.

He shuddered against her and groaned. One great thrust and he came into her, spurting his hot essence into the heart of her. She grew wet with his juices, feeling him slip and slide into her as he continued to thrust. She'd never felt anything as erotic as her skin rubbing against his, and with a wild cry of surprise she felt herself come again.

It was all-consuming, this passion. This lust. This intense need. Enya didn't understand how it could have happened so quickly. Her body belonged to his in a way it had never belonged to anyone before. No lover had ever made her feel so much sheer sensation. Only John. He had been able to make her feel so incredible that she'd forgotten all her troubles.

She came down from the heavens and found herself resting on top of John—he had rolled them to keep his weight from crushing her. His wide chest cushioned her head as he held her to him. Her legs fell between his, and his hands stroked her from head to bottom, petting her like he might a kitten.

Within minutes, Enya was so relaxed that she drifted off to sleep.

Chapter Seven

ﾛ

When Enya awoke, it was dark in the cabin. Only a shaft of moonlight pierced through the windows to cast eerie shadows in the blackness. Enya pulled away from John's still-cradling arms, careful not to wake him, and went to the kitchen for a cup of water.

Her body felt fuzzy and warm, aching only slightly when she walked. Her nipples were hard in the cool night air, still dusky and rouged from John's kiss.

She drank her water with a thirst that didn't surprise her after such exertion in her lover's arms. Some of it dribbled out of the corner of her mouth, she drank it so fast, and it trailed down over her breasts, teasing her as John's fingers had teased her.

Enya walked back to the couch and looked down at him, trying to see through the shadows. A shaft of moonlight fell over his mouth—and the memories that had dogged her since meeting John clicked together in her mind.

"Motherfucker!" she shouted, pulling on his hair to wake him.

"What the hell?" He shot off the couch in a flash. "What's going on? Are you okay?"

"Okay? Am I *okay*? No, I'm not okay for fuck's sake! God damn you, you lying sack of shit." She mimicked his voice, "'He's bad news and you should stay away from him', weren't those your exact words?"

"What are you talking about?" he growled, taking her shoulders in his hands and shaking her.

"You know exactly what I'm talking about," she raged. "You're Johnny Vicious!"

John caught his breath and shook her again. "Don't you tease me like this, I won't stand for it."

"You won't stand for it? God, what an asshole! You need to worry about what *I'll* stand for now that I know who you are. I could report you to the police and they'd pick you up in a second."

"I'm *not* Johnny Vicious," he protested.

Enya caught the inflection in his voice that said he wasn't entirely convinced by his own lie.

"I recognized your mouth. No one has a mouth like you. You *are* Vicious, admit it."

"I think you've been under too much stress. You're thinking crazy things."

"You think *I'm* crazy?" she thundered.

"I won't discuss this further." John jerked his pants on, not even bothering with his boxers. "I'm leaving," he said. "I need some time alone."

"You can't leave me here," she growled.

"I won't be gone long. I just have to think."

"Fine, be that way. *Leave.*" She turned and walked to the bedroom, uncaring of her nudity, and slammed the door shut.

A few minutes later she heard the sound of John's patrol car. He revved the engine and his tires spat gravel as he pulled away.

"Damn it," she huffed, and threw herself onto the bed.

* * * * *

John rubbed a hand over his face as he sped down the gravel road away from the cabin. Nothing made any sense to him anymore, and he was in a rage because of it.

Was he Johnny Vicious? Was that why he kept waking up in strange places? Was that why he was so familiar with the seedy underbelly of Cleveland? For the past year he'd been catching perps left and right, as if he'd known exactly where to look for them. Could this be why?

He didn't know.

It was that simple. And because he didn't know, he feared that it was so. But how? How could he be Vicious and not know it? The answer to that was too terrifying to dwell upon.

He pulled out onto the main road and let the lines that dotted it hypnotize him into a state of calm. The gray haze took him and everything else faded away.

* * * * *

Enya felt hands stroking her hair and woke with a start.

"Hello, pretty eyes," Johnny Vicious said as he sat upon the edge of her bed. "We need to talk."

Enya pulled the sheet up to cover her breasts.

"I think it's a little late for that now," he said darkly.

"So you're admitting you're Johnny Vicious?" she demanded.

"I *am* Johnny Vicious, but I don't think John can accept it quite yet."

"What the hell are you talking about?"

Johnny pushed the hat back on his head, revealing his light green eyes. "You saw how dazed John was when you confronted him. He doesn't know that we are, in fact, the same person. But he's starting to suspect."

Enya gaped at him. "But you *are* John."

"Technically, yes."

"What the hell do you mean, 'technically'?"

"We share the same body but not the same space of mind."

She shook her head to clear it. "I don't understand how that can be."

Johnny smiled slowly and Enya had to fight to keep her pulse steady. "I'm his alter ego. Another personality entirely.

John has no idea when I take control. He simply blacks out and there I am."

"I can't believe this," she whispered, shaken.

"I don't think you should discuss me anymore with John. I seem to upset him."

"Gee, I wonder why," Enya said, moving back away from him.

"I'm not going to hurt you. Don't be afraid."

"How can I *not* be afraid? You're talking about split personalities here. I can't even begin to understand how to handle this situation!"

"John isn't ready to face me yet. He's under enough stress taking care of you."

"How can he face you?! You're the same person," she shrieked.

"He will have to acknowledge me sooner or later, but he's just not ready yet."

"How do you know so much about him while he knows so little about you?"

"I made it a point to study my alter ego extensively. While I don't know everything that he knows, I do have some ideas. For instance, I know he's never come so hard inside a woman as he did inside of you."

Enya gasped. "You crass asshole."

"I can't help it. I've had a hard-on for you since I first saw you. All that dark hair and cinnamon skin just drives me wild. It's no surprise to me that John likes you too."

Enya shivered, his words seducing some primitive side of her despite her anger and shock.

"I can still smell you on my skin," he whispered sinfully.

"Stop it," she protested.

"Stop what?" he drawled, voice smoky and deep.

"Stop this, stop trying to throw me off balance."

"Was that what I was doing? And here I thought I was seducing you."

"No," she gritted. "No, you can't seduce me. Not now."

"But I can have fun trying, right?"

"Shut up. Let me think. I don't know up from down anymore."

"I felt much the same way the first time I came through John. But you'll get used to it. I have, and hell only knows I'm in a precarious position to say the least."

"How did this happen?" she asked.

"I don't know exactly how. One day I was just there, split from John as if I'd been born somebody different. John was growing tired of law enforcement—he'd seen too many bad guys get away with their crimes. I came out and found a way to make sure the perps don't get away."

"You kill them."

Johnny started. "No. I just hogtie them red-handed and wait for the cops to show up. It's up to John to sort out the rest of the legalities. I'm a vigilante, not a murderer. You read my card." He smiled.

"Do you always leave your calling card with those you save?" she asked.

"Yes. It's the only mark I can leave behind. Plus, I like the absurdity of carrying around business cards in John's favorite coat. He's found them a couple of times and now he almost never sticks his hands in his pockets. Watch him, you'll notice it right away, how he avoids his pockets."

"I've never seen him wear that coat."

"I usually keep it folded in my briefcase along with my guns and hat."

"No you don't, I've seen what's in that briefcase. There are just some papers and John's Beretta."

"There's a secret compartment. And only I know the combination to it," Johnny drawled.

"Show me," she demanded.

Johnny rose and left the room. He came back some minutes later with the unusually large, unusually thick silver briefcase. He laid it on the bed and twisted the combination numbers to read 777—the number of heaven. The briefcase fell open, revealing a hidden compartment that took up nearly the entire breadth of the case.

"Hasn't John ever noticed how thick this thing is? How heavy?"

"John only notices what he wants to when it comes to things concerning me and my doings."

"I can't believe all this," she said. "It's too much to take in. I feel like I'm going crazy."

"Welcome to the club," he chuckled.

She choked off a laugh with some surprise. She hadn't known she could laugh at a time like this. What a strange night this had turned out to be, and after such a promising day.

"Well, I'm off. John will be wanting to get back to you. He worries, you see."

She frowned. "And you don't."

"Guilty. I am the part of John that can be totally free. Worrying just wastes time, if you ask me." He picked up the briefcase and walked to her door. He paused. "Be gentle with John, if you can. He's going through a lot right now."

"And I'm not?"

"You can handle it."

"Are you saying John can't?"

"I'm here, aren't I? I think that speaks for itself just how well John can handle stress."

This time Enya did laugh, but she felt immediate guilt.

"Don't feel too bad," he said, as if reading her mind. "John's a tough cookie. I'm just tougher, that's all." With that he left her, his motions a blur in the night.

How the hell did he move like that?

The question plagued her the rest of her sleepless night.

Chapter Eight
The next morning

෨

John served her scrambled eggs in silence.

"Won't you talk to me?" she asked at last. "We don't have to talk about last night if you don't want to."

He plopped down in the chair opposite her. "I bought you some bubble bath," he said at great length. "It's jasmine scented, I hope that's okay."

A bubble bath sounded lovely, especially since she was still aching between her legs. "That's very okay," she said, and meant it.

"Did you sleep all right last night?"

"No."

"Me neither. I think."

John's cell phone rang and Enya jumped. John looked at the caller I.D. "It's the chief," he said and answered on the next ring.

Enya wandered back into her bedroom. She wondered what the next step would be. How she could bridge the gap that had grown between her and John. She knew she shouldn't talk about Johnny, but she couldn't think of anything else.

John's mind was broken. It was two pieces of a whole, but each side unique in its own way. How could she help him? How could she bring the two halves together? Was that even possible? She needed to get home to her computer and do some extensive research to find out more.

Plus, she had to know how Johnny Vicious could move like he did and still be human. Enya had never seen anyone move that fast, not by half. She didn't know how it was even physiologically possible.

She sat on her bed—and the walls exploded around her.

Machine gun fire, heavy and fast, assailed the house. It tore though the walls as if they were made of paper, not wood. Enya cried out and threw herself flat onto the floor as splinters and glass flew around her.

"Enya!" John flew into the room and fell down beside her. "Are you hurt?" he asked.

"No," she yelled as another spray of bullets tore into the room.

"Come on," he said and grabbed her arms, literally lifting her up off the floor. A bullet whizzed by John's ear but he gave it no notice as he half dragged, half carried her into the sitting room.

"How did they find us?" she wailed.

"God damn it, they must have seen me and followed me back last night."

"Shit," she said. "And I was just beginning to get used to this place."

Her weak attempt at humor did nothing to faze him, so intent was he to get her to safety.

"How can we escape?" she asked.

"We're going to go out the front door."

"Are you *nuts*? We'll be killed."

His green eyes blazed, gaze holding hers steady. "No we won't," he said with steel in his voice.

He grabbed his briefcase from beside the couch and set the combination to 187, a common police code for homicide. He took his handgun out and closed the case with a click. A bullet came screaming into the sitting room, and John barely moved Enya away in time. It whizzed past both of them, breaking a lamp with a shattering of glass. John turned and fired, tracing the bullet's trajectory back to its source.

There came a loud grunt and Enya knew John had hit his target.

"Come on," he said and grabbed the briefcase, ushering her out the door.

Bullets flew past them but John always seemed one step ahead, dodging them with a grace and flare that reminded her entirely of Vicious. He fired his gun into the trees, laying down a path of bullets that cleared their way to John's patrol car.

He practically thrust her into the front seat and slid over the hood of the car to reach the driver's side. He tossed the briefcase into the backseat and cranked the car, slamming his door. He threw the car into drive and took off, spitting a cloud of gravel in their wake.

The car bounced and shuddered as they gained speed and hit pits and rocks in the road. The back glass shattered and Enya screamed. She looked behind them and saw the same truck that had run them down a few days ago, hot on their trail.

"God damn it, take the wheel," John said.

Enya had no choice but to take control of the car when John slipped into the backseat. She grabbed the wheel and slid over to the driver's side. She had a little trouble steering at first, but she mastered it quickly, guiding the car on the twisting road away from the cottage.

John fired his gun out the shattered back window, aiming for the truck's tires. The driver of the truck spun to the left wildly but came back and returned fire. Enya ducked, as if that would stop a bullet from hitting her, and pressed the gas pedal to the floor.

They exploded out onto the four-lane highway going the wrong way, but luckily there was no traffic to dodge. Enya picked up speed and soon the truck began to lose ground against them. John reloaded his gun and fired out the back window again, and this time he struck his target. The truck spun wildly off the road, flipped and landed on the grassy median.

"Don't stop, just keep going," John told her.

"I have to turn around," she said and braked sharply, spinning the car into a one-hundred-and-eighty-degree turn.

She sped back past the truck and couldn't resist gawking. It had landed on its top. There was no movement from the people within it, but Enya wasn't ready to hang around and wait for the survivors to appear. She left the truck in their dust, driving away as fast as the car would carry them.

* * * * *

Four hours later

The hotel was quiet, with very few visitors. It wasn't a lavish affair but it was comfortable, and Enya was grateful for that. She plopped down upon one of the double beds with a heavy sigh and watched as John settled his briefcase into a chair.

"We'll be safe here until I can think of another place to take you," he said in a rough, strained voice.

"What's wrong?" she asked, concerned.

John's eyes darkened. "I put you in danger by leaving last night. I led them back to you. All because I let my temper get the best of me. I'm sorry."

"Don't be sorry," she said. "We got away. We'll be safe now, like you said. Besides, those guys are probably busted up pretty bad. They won't be able to bother us for a little while."

"Siren really wants you out of the picture."

"Yeah." She closed her eyes and fell back upon the bed.

"I won't let them hurt you," he said hoarsely.

"I know," she said.

He reclined next to her on the bed and folded his arms around her, holding her tight. She let him hold her, resting her head on his chest, calmed by the steady beating of his heart in her ear. Soon she was lulled into a doze against him.

* * * * *

Enya woke up some time later to a dark room, which startled her for she hadn't turned off any of the lights. And, to confuse matters more, she was nude in the bed.

John stirred against her back, his lips exploring the nape of her neck, and she settled herself against him, wanting more of the caress. His hand came around her and cupped her breast. Her nipple immediately hardened and she moaned softly.

His hand moved down to her leg and he brought it back to hook over his. He positioned his body between her legs and pressed his hot, hard cock against her already damp pussy. He stroked her leg and rubbed his cock in her wetness, thrusting his hips against her over and over.

Enya shivered in his arms. His lips moved over her shoulder, questing softly, mouth hot. She moved back against him and moaned again, seeking a deeper embrace. "Fuck me, John. Fuck me so hard I forget everything else," she begged.

He positioned his cock against her and paused. "The name's Johnny," he said softly, and thrust into her.

Enya cried out and tried to pull out of the embrace, but Johnny held her tight, his body a part of hers. "Shhh," he cajoled. "Do you feel me inside of you? That's where I belong. When I'm inside of you it feels like coming home." He thrust into her again, his hips cradling hers.

She couldn't help but melt against him.

Johnny's hand petted the front of her, focusing on her breasts and belly then moving down to play with her pussy. Enya gasped and moved into his touch, taking his cock deeper as she did so. His fingers found her clit and she moaned as he rubbed and squeezed the hard kernel of flesh.

The next second, he turned her in the bed, laying her on her stomach. He put a pillow under her hips to raise her to him and thrust into her body balls deep. His hands squeezed the globes of her ass until she cried out at the sting. He slapped her bottom and she moaned, her body turning liquid. He spanked her again and began to ride her.

Her bottom was hot and stinging. Her pussy was stretched beyond limits. And she desperately wanted more.

Johnny put one of his fingers in her mouth and she sucked on it. Then he took that same finger away and a moment later slid it into the tight ring of her anus. Enya shrieked and bucked against him, but he continued to ride her, his cock filling her pussy, his finger filling her ass.

He touched something deep inside of her, reaching it with every thrust he made. He slapped her ass again and she came with a scream. As she spasmed around his cock, he began thrusting his finger in and out of her anus. Her climax then took her higher than she'd ever been before.

Time seemed to slow. Enya looked about her and noticed a tiny fly, floating in the air. She saw every single beat of its wings, every nuance of its movements. Johnny's movements seemed to slow with time as well, his body moving gracefully into hers, like a dance. Like the tides of the ocean.

Her release was absolute. Enya sobbed with the force of it, twisting in his arms, but he held her fast and rode her through it. A moment later he groaned and filled her pussy with his hot, creamy cum.

After it was over he collapsed onto her, pressing her deep into the mattress.

"God, that was amazing," Johnny murmured with awe.

Enya wholeheartedly agreed with him.

It took her several minutes to find her voice again.

"What are you doing here, Johnny?"

"Fucking you," he chuckled.

Enya rolled out from under him and pulled out of his embrace. "I noticed that much," she said cheekily.

"Good. I wouldn't want to have to prove myself again so soon," he grinned.

Enya looked at him and for the first time saw the hat he wore. Despite their exercise, he hadn't lost it. "Do you always wear your hat, Johnny?"

"Always. John hates wearing hats. I like them. Or I guess I should say that I'm particularly fond of this one."

"Why are you so fond of it?" she asked.

"It was my grandfather's," he answered. Then he frowned. "Or John's grandfather's. Whatever."

It occurred to her how bizarre this situation really was and she told him so. "This is too much for me right now," she grumbled, only half meaning it, her body still aglow with the heat of her orgasm.

Johnny rose, his body beautiful in all its nude glory, and took her chin in his hand. "I haven't kissed you tonight, pretty eyes." He leaned down and whispered his lips over hers. "And I do love kissing you."

Enya opened her mouth to his and let his tongue slide in along hers. Their tongues danced and dueled, his flavor buzzing in her mind like a heady wine. There came again that feeling of time slowing to a crawl. She pulled away to ask what was happening when he pushed her back onto the bed, and took her beneath him once again.

He slid into her easily and gently began to thrust. They mated in silence, their mouths locked together as one. When his tongue filled her, so too did his cock. His hands roamed all over her body, bringing her to the brink again.

He pulled at her nipples with his fingers, pinching and squeezing them so that Enya moaned her arousal aloud. He plumped and massaged the fullness of her breasts and rocked into her harder, the bed beginning to protest with squeaks and creaks.

Johnny rose up over her, his green gaze holding hers captive. "Look at me when you come," he commanded in a wicked whisper. "Don't take your eyes off mine."

Thrust and withdrawal. Thrust and withdrawal. Enya began to breathe in time with the primitive rhythm their bodies made. She felt her body quiver beneath his hands. Her heart thundered a savage beat in her breast. Her body felt strung like the tightest bow.

Her release came on slow but took her hard. She felt her body pulse and milk around his great girth. Her head swam with the sensation. Her eyes watered. Her nipples felt hard as diamonds beneath his hands. She moaned deeply, her body shuddering beneath his, and went weak with release.

"Don't close your eyes," he commanded, and her lids flew open, her gaze locking with his.

He continued to rock into her. Then he groaned and grimaced, his face hardening to stone as he came within her body. There came that eerie slowing of time again, his cum filling her for what seemed an eternity. His eyes never left hers.

"Do you see?" he breathed.

She saw. Everything seemed to be moving in slow motion about them. "I see," she answered with a moan.

Time came crashing down and they both collapsed into the mattress.

Sweetest oblivion took her down into an exhausted sleep and she didn't wake until morning.

Chapter Nine
The next day

છ

"So let me get this straight. To keep me safe, I'm to be taken back to my apartment where I was attacked?" she asked, incredulous.

"The FBI is taking this more seriously now. You'll have two guards at all times. You'll be escorted everywhere you go. I don't think there'll be another attempt on your life, if that gives you any confidence."

"You don't think—*John*! These are the same people who tracked us down to a little knothole cabin in the woods. Of course they'll try again if I go back. Siren wants me dead and they'll stop at nothing to make it so. I can't believe you're going to take me back."

"Those are my orders," he said stonily.

Enya gritted her teeth then nodded. "I understand. You're ready to get back to your life."

"It's not like that," he protested.

"It's okay. I know it can't be fun dragging a marked woman around with you everywhere."

"Enya. Stop it. Right now. I won't be leaving you. I'll be there with you as long as you want me. But this is the FBI's territory now. I won't have much say in what happens to you. They told me to bring you back, and bring you back I must."

"They're going to kill me, John!" she exclaimed.

"No they're not."

"Vicious wouldn't take me back," she said, and immediately regretted it.

John's jaw clenched. "Don't you dare bring him up. Don't you dare."

"He was here last night," she said, wanting him to hurt as much as she did. "He fucked me over and over."

John stepped close and shook her. "He wasn't here last night. I slept in that bed next to you. *I* did. Not Vicious."

She let him subside a little and heard herself ask with some surprise and no small amount of regret, "Don't you wonder which one of you fucks me better?"

"God damn it woman, I refuse to discuss this foolishness with you anymore."

"Why are you so afraid to face the truth?"

"There *is* no truth in this, only craziness!" he cried.

Enya subsided. Several minutes passed. "I'm sorry I said that, John," she apologized.

"Which thing are you apologizing for?" He grabbed his briefcase and made for the door.

"For all of it." Enya followed him out, wincing at the pouring rain.

John was silent for a moment as he settled them into his badly damaged patrol car. "I'm sorry for yelling at you," he said, turning to face her. "Look, I don't like this any better than you, if you want the truth of it. I'd rather take you someplace secret and guard you there. But I can't. My orders are that I'm to take you back home and that's exactly what I'm going to do. I'm sorry, but that's the way it has to be."

Enya nodded. "I know. Let's go. We've got a long drive ahead of us."

* * * * *

Three days later

John was frantic to see Enya again. He hadn't been allowed a moment's peace to do it in, though. He'd had so much paperwork to fill out once he returned that his head nearly swam. But he was determined that tonight he'd go see her.

What must she be thinking? That he'd abandoned her? That he'd lost interest? Nothing could have been further from the truth.

He wanted to call her, but the FBI was taping all of her calls. What he had to say to her was not for curious ears.

Somehow, despite the danger, they had bonded in a way John had never experienced. He found himself liking all sorts of things about her. The way her hair fell around her shoulders, the way she stuck her tongue out when she was concentrating, her courage and determination to do the right thing even when facing insurmountable odds. She was a marvel to him. Brave and strong and highly opinionated. She was perfect.

He needed her. He knew it. He'd never felt so calm and relaxed as he had in her presence and he sorely missed that peace. Something about her resonated with him, took away his worries and cares. She made him strong. She made him whole.

He regretted not kissing her. He'd kissed his way over most of her body, but somehow he's forgotten her lips. He planned to rectify that tonight. He'd kiss her for hours if she'd let him.

God. How he wanted her!

But there was this matter of Johnny Vicious. He was like a ghost come between them.

John didn't want to remember all the times he'd awakened to find himself in a strange place. In a strange situation. With no memory of how he'd gotten there. He'd been angry with Enya for confronting him about Vicious, but he'd been even angrier with himself for not knowing the truth.

If he told her how confused he'd been this past year, maybe she'd understand and help him work through it. He didn't want to believe he was a vigilante, but the proof was damning.

Enya had said Vicious had taken her. And John had wanted her to recant it. But he'd smelled her on his skin and known that something had happened between them that he had no recollection of. Or between Enya and Johnny. It was all too confusing—he couldn't begin to sort it all out.

He promised himself that he would try. It was all he could do.

* * * * *

Enya opened the door for John and invited him in. She hadn't heard from him in three days. She'd wanted to call him, but her phone was tapped and what she had to say to him wasn't meant for others to hear.

She'd missed him.

She'd wondered if he'd lost interest. God, she'd nearly eaten her heart out with the thought. She felt sorry that she'd confronted him about Vicious. She wanted to help him sort his life—or lives—out. She wanted Spada and Vicious to become one.

There were things about both men that she liked. John's steadfast nerves and clear-headed thinking in a crisis. Johnny's wit and style. It was hard to believe that they were the same man at times.

Enya wondered how she could help him realize the truth about who he was.

She was falling in love, but she didn't know if it was Johnny Vicious or John Spada that she was falling for. This confusion rattled her. She couldn't begin to imagine how John must feel about it.

And now, finally, he was here in her home with her.

"What took you so long?" she asked cheekily.

John smiled and held out a bouquet of flowers for her to take. "How have you been doing?"

"I'm feeling like a caged bird right now," she said. "I haven't left this place in three days. I'm beginning to forget what the outside world is like." She chuckled.

"Rainy," John said with a smile. "You're not missing much, believe me."

"I missed you," she said softly.

John took her in his arms and held her tight. "I came as soon as I could. I had to make statements regarding the attacks and then I had a mountain of paperwork to fill out." He sighed. "I missed you too, baby doll. So much."

"Can we just skip this date and hop in the sack?" she murmured against his chest.

John was surprised into laughter. "Who said I wanted a date with you?" he teased.

"Come on," she said and led him to the bedroom.

Once there, she turned and let her hands roam to the fastening of his uniform. She bared his chest to her hands and stroked him hungrily. She put her mouth to one of his dusky nipples and she reveled in how still and intense John suddenly became.

"Will you fuck me in this uniform?" she asked coyly.

John shivered and let out a big breath. "If you want me to, I'll *make love* to you in my uniform."

"Make love, yes. That too." Enya chuckled and let her hands catch in the fastening of his trousers. She reached past them into his boxers and pulled out his massive cock, stroking him.

She dropped to her knees before him and looked up into his waiting gaze. "Watch me when you come," she commanded.

He shuddered and tangled his hands in her hair as she dipped and licked his cock from crown to base. She cupped his sac and sucked it into her mouth gently. John moaned, hands spasming, watching her every movement. Watching her tongue dart out to lave his shaft. Watching her hands pump and stroke his turgid length.

He was so thick and wide that she couldn't fit more than the head of his cock within her mouth. But she suckled and worshipped him there until he was shaking against her. He bucked his hips against her, forcing more of his flesh into her mouth. Enya suckled him deep, careful to keep her teeth away from him.

She masturbated him with her hands while she sucked on his cock head like she would a lollipop. John groaned and moved with her, humping her hands and mouth with mindless abandon.

Enya felt his cock spasm in her mouth and she opened wide to swallow his cum. He spurted hard into her mouth, hot and creamy and wet. She swallowed his seed, licking the hole in his cock to drain him completely. Not a drop was lost to her.

John caught his breath and jerked her up to her feet. Enya kissed him, letting him taste his own flavor on her tongue. John growled and ripped at her clothing. Within seconds she was nude and he had her back against the wall. He lifted her, letting her wrap her legs around his waist, and pressed his semi-hard member into her.

He felt softer now, not so demanding inside her body. She sank down on him with a long exhalation of breath. He pressed her tight to the wall and looked into her eyes. "You feel great," he said.

Enya laughed. "You too," she answered.

He began to bounce her on his dick, making her moan. Wet, sucking noises filled their ears as, with each thrust, her body greedily tried to keep him inside. Her breasts rubbed against his bare chest, her nipples stabbing demandingly into his skin.

His hands came around her and cupped her ass, lifting her into each thrust of his body. His hands burned her there, squeezing and kneading her tender flesh so that she cried out and rode him harder. Their skin slapped together as she galloped toward the finish.

She came with a keening cry, clutching him to her, sobbing with the force of her release.

He lowered her to the floor and she would have fallen if he wasn't there to catch her. He withdrew from her body as she slid down, causing them both to shiver deliciously. He took her up in his arms, like a babe, and walked her to the bed, laying her down upon it gently. He lay down next to her and cuddled her, spooning her, as their breathing slowed.

"That was incredible," she said in awe.

"Yes it was," he agreed wholeheartedly, holding her tight as if he'd never let her go again.

Chapter Ten

ಐ

Enya awoke the moment John put his mouth on her pussy. His tongue moved through the seam of her sex like liquid. He spread her open wide and pressed a hard kiss to her clit.

Enya bucked against him and he laughed wickedly.

He sucked the bud of her clit into his mouth and teased it with the tip of his tongue. Enya moaned and let her hands catch in his silky hair. He licked her like he would an ice cream cone, lapping up an entirely different sort of cream. Within seconds she was so wet that his mouth barely kept up with her.

"Ride my mouth." He whispered the words into her tender, needy flesh. "Let me know you want it."

He thrust a long, hard finger into her and continued to lick and kiss and nibble his way up and down her pussy. He lifted her up higher against his face then spread her bottom and licked her anus. Enya shrieked and convulsed around his finger.

She moved against him, bucked and arched and undulated until she was mindless with need. He slipped two more fingers into her, stretching her, and she sobbed her desire, begging him to take her.

"Please take me, John. Fuck me, love me, make me come," she babbled, hardly knowing what she was saying anymore.

He rose up between her legs, removed his hand from her body and licked her cream from his fingers. He lifted the head of his cock, laying it at her opening. Then, with a fierce, hard lunge, he was inside of her.

He thrust quick and hard, over and over, until Enya was crazed with lust. The headboard of the bed banged against the wall as they raced into the heights of passion. He stretched her until she burned, and filled her up until she ached.

She came with a scream.

When she came back to herself she heard a loud knocking on her door.

"Are you all right, Ms. Merritt?" called one of her guards through the door.

Enya burned crimson with embarrassment. "Y-yes," she stammered. "I, uh, stubbed my toe."

John laughed into the crook of her neck.

"Just call us if you need us," the guard said, his tone stating clearly that he knew *exactly* what she'd been up to.

"Come on, baby doll," John said, rising and offering her his hand. "Let's take this to the shower."

* * * * *

Enya eyed John's briefcase warily as he was busy wandering about her kitchen, finding them something to eat. She reached out and set the combination to 777 and opened it gently.

The case held Johnny's two enormous handguns, his hat and his coat, all tightly packed within its confines.

Enya gasped and shut the case again, but seeing these things didn't shock her as much as she'd thought it might.

Minutes later John came and sat next to her on the sofa with two roast beef sandwiches. "What's wrong baby doll, you look like you've seen a ghost."

Enya debated over her words carefully before she spoke. "We need to talk about Johnny Vicious," she said.

John sighed heavily. "I know," he said, and reached out to play with a lock of her hair. "I don't want to but I know we have to."

"Do you want proof that you're Johnny?" she asked, gesturing to the briefcase.

John clenched his jaw. "There's no need. I believe you. I don't understand how this could be, but I believe you."

Enya reached for one of his hands. "How long have you been like this?" she asked.

"About a year, I think. That's when I started having blackouts, losing time. Are you scared?"

"I'm scared *for* you, not *of* you," she said, answering his real question. "But what I don't understand is how, when you're Johnny, you can move as fast as you do."

"I don't know what you're talking about," he frowned.

"Johnny moves so fast it's like he's not even human. He dodges bullets. He can walk between raindrops, he's that fast."

"I'm perfectly human, I assure you. Fucked up in the head, but still human." At least he hoped so.

"Can you move that fast now?" she asked.

John shook his head. "I'm fast enough, I have good reflexes, but I'm not as fast as you say Johnny is." He tried not to think about the one time he'd somehow become aware while in 'Johnny mode'. It seemed so long ago now anyway, he knew he couldn't remember everything clearly. Had he moved like Johnny then, before blacking out again? He wasn't certain anymore.

"Maybe you should go to a doctor, maybe there's a physiological reason for it."

"No. No way am I going to let a doctor tinker around in my head. It's bad enough that you're doing it." He smiled to soften his words. "Besides, the scientists at Sterling have already been studying me."

"Maybe Johnny knows what we should do," she said, and reached for the briefcase again. "Let's ask him."

John shot up off the couch. "No. I can't just bring him out like that. I have no control over it. I don't even begin to know how to go about it."

"I think I know what will bring him out," she said, and set the combination once more to 777.

When she opened the case, John went white beneath his tan. "How are those in there? I only keep my papers in there."

"It's a secret compartment Johnny showed me. Haven't you ever wondered why it's so damned heavy?"

"Well yeah, but I didn't give it much thought," he admitted.

Enya took out the crumpled bootlegger's hat, rose from the couch and reached to put it on John's head.

"What the hell are you doing?"

"I'm trying something. Don't worry. Everything will be all right."

"I don't like this, Enya."

"I'll be here if you need me. Promise. I won't run away," she said with what she hoped was a comforting smile.

She set the hat on top of his head and waited.

Nothing happened.

"Nothing's happening," John said.

Enya lifted the hat then brought it down back over his head, hard. "Johnny, are you in there?" she asked, looking into John's eyes as if she would see his alter ego in their depths.

John jerked against her and she gasped.

She watched his face go vacant and slack. His hands hung lifelessly at his side. His eyes hooded heavily. He was still breathing, that much Enya could see, but he was no longer there with her. John had left the building.

Slowly, by small degrees, his face filled with life again. He jerked hard and nearly fell. He blinked once, twice, a third time.

And he looked out at her with that debonair, cocksure flare she'd come to expect from Johnny.

The switch had only taken a few minutes.

"Johnny?" she asked, to be sure.

"That's me, pretty eyes. So you know my secret? All the magic's always in the clothes you know," he teased.

"If I take the hat off, John will come back, won't he?"

Johnny grinned and plopped down onto the couch, leaving her to stand, propping his feet up and biting hungrily into John's sandwich. "Right again, my dear. Ugh, this has mayonnaise on it." He put the sandwich back on the plate.

"I want to ask you something," she started.

"Ask away," he said and took a swig from John's cola.

"How do you move so fast? Dodging bullets and almost disappearing before my eyes, that sort of thing."

Johnny smiled. "Time slows for me when I get an adrenaline rush. It's something I've been able to do from the first time I came out of John. Time slows for me but stays constant for you, so when you see me running or moving fast, your eyes can barely keep up with me."

"How do you know this while John doesn't? How can you do this while John can't?"

"The easy explanation is that John's always had this power inside of him. But it took me to bring it out of him. He's stubborn, our John."

"I'm going to take the hat off now," she said.

He rose from the couch and approached her. "One thing before I go," he said and bent to take her lips with his.

Enya felt his mouth slide over hers like hot silk. His tongue spilled into her mouth, his flavor making her head spin. He clutched her tight to him, raising her up so that her lower belly cuddled against his erection.

He eased back and let his lips whisper back and forth across hers. "So, do we make love the same, John and I?" he asked.

Enya started. "Yes," she said. "Yes you do."

He grinned. "Good. I'm glad the old boy finally got something right." He reached up and took the hat off, tossing it to her.

His face went slack again, his eyes vacant. Enya tried not to turn away from his ghostly pallor, his emotionless face. His eyes blinked, so fast she would have missed it if she hadn't been watching him so closely. Slowly but surely life began to infuse his face and form once more.

A minute later and John had returned.

"Did you miss me?" she asked, eyes brimming with tears, aching for his plight.

John smiled sadly. "I did."

Chapter Eleven
One week later

∞

"Ms. Merritt, there's someone here to meet you," Argyle, one of her guards, told her. "He's clean, we checked him out."

"Let him in please," she smiled. She liked Argyle, which had surprised her at first. She'd expected to be very shy of her new guards, considering what had happened with the last one. But she'd adapted quickly. Somewhat.

John had helped her with that. He no longer spent his nights out doing goodness knows what. He spent them in her bed. Johnny Vicious had been absent now for a week.

A tall blond man entered her apartment. "Ms. Enya Merritt?"

Enya nodded, eyeing him suspiciously.

"My name is Ryan Murdock." He offered her a business card. "I head a governmental project called Sterling. May we sit and talk?"

Enya nodded. "Would you like anything to drink?"

"No thank you. I don't think I'll be here long." Ryan cleared his throat. "I understand that we share an acquaintance, you and I."

Enya frowned. "Yeah?"

"John Spada. AKA Johnny Vicious."

Enya started violently. "H-how do you know about—"

"Vicious? I guess you could say that I'm part of the reason there even *is* a Johnny Vicious."

"I don't understand."

"Allow me to explain. About a year ago, we conducted a sleep-deprivation experiment with some of the local law enforcement. John Spada was one of the test subjects."

"He hasn't said anything about that."

"He probably doesn't remember it. Besides, it wasn't just sleep-deprivation we were studying. We were searching through Cleveland's finest officers. We were looking for the right sort of test subject to advance to the next level of the program. John was the perfect candidate for it. We saw that right away."

"What happened?"

"A split in his personality, as you have seen. The tests were grueling. John went for days without rest, going through exercise after exercise until he collapsed. When he woke up, he was Johnny."

"I thought he needed his hat to be Johnny?" she said, shaken.

"That has become a physical switch for him to change alters. He uses it more metaphorically than anything else, I think. But as Johnny he excelled in his tests, proving us right about John. John has an extrasensory power, one we call Time Chasing. And it became clear to us that John couldn't face this power, that only Johnny could command it."

"You fucked around with his head!" she raged. "How could you do something like that to a human being?"

"I don't expect you to understand right away what our program is all about."

"You broke his mind and let him run loose after you'd finished with him."

"No, we've never lost contact with him," he said calmly in the face of her anger.

"What do you mean?"

"Where do you think Johnny got his guns? Why do you think he goes out every night to take the law into his own hands? He reports to us. We help him use his powers in the best way possible, give him assignments. Drug dealers, rapists, child molesters—all the people who have slipped down into the cracks of the judicial system, we make sure they don't get away with their crimes. We send Johnny—and others like him—out to catch them in their acts of treachery. It's what our program is all about—saving humanity from itself."

Enya eyed him warily, her heart beating with a rage she'd never before felt. "You took the man I love and broke him. Why are you here telling me this?"

"So you do love him? I had suspected as much between you two." He mulled it over. "As for your question, Johnny hasn't checked in for a whole week. He's never gone so long without contacting us. We need to check and make sure everything is all right."

"Get out," she snapped. "John's not here, and even if he were, I wouldn't let you see him."

"I think you should ask *him* about it before you decide, don't you? We can help John become whole again if that's what he wants, or we can continue as we have to this point. We won't leave him cut adrift, so to speak. We take care of our own," Ryan said stonily.

"I'm in the middle of a big spot of trouble, in case the FBI agents guarding my door escaped your notice. John's having his own trouble keeping his head straight. I don't want you to mess things up further."

"We can keep you safe too, if that is what you want. We are far beyond Siren's reach, believe me. You and John could come and stay in our compound, with your own condo, your own private lives. We don't want anything bad to happen to either of you."

"Why?"

"Because you are obviously so important to John. Therefore you're important to us too."

Enya watched him in silence. "Can you really help him?" she asked in a hoarse, strained voice.

Ryan smiled gently and Enya was surprised to notice how attractive he looked with his bright blond hair, tanned skin and all-American blue eyes. "We can help you both."

"I'll take care of myself. But if you can help John...I'll ask him what he thinks, okay?"

"That would be great." He rose from his seat and gave her a tiny bow. "You have my card. You know how to reach me when you're ready."

He disappeared before she could reply, vanishing before her very eyes, with a strange popping noise as he went.

* * * * *

Enya had a tough time explaining Ryan Murdock's disappearance to Argyle. He didn't believe her when she lied and told him Ryan had left out her third-story window, taking the rusted fire escape that probably couldn't hold the weight of a pigeon, but she couldn't think up a better lie. And he certainly wouldn't have believed the truth.

She hardly did herself.

Argyle searched her house thoroughly before he was convinced that somehow Ryan Murdock had left without his notice. When he was satisfied with his search he went back to his post, in a chair outside her door with Elliott, her other guard for the day. She might have asked them in to play cards, but she was still a little too skittish after her previous run-in with the FBI.

So she bided her time until John arrived, which he did at exactly eight o'clock.

She watched him as they ate her spaghetti and wondered just how much he might remember from Ryan Murdock's so-called program.

She decided to find out.

"I had a visitor today," she said carefully.

John frowned. "Who was it?"

"A man named Ryan Murdock. He says he knows you. Does the name ring any bells?"

John's face paled, but he rallied quickly. "It does, but I don't know why. What did he have to say?"

Enya debated long and hard about how she should proceed next. She decided it was best to tell him the truth. "He knows about you and Johnny. He knows why and how you split into these two halves. He says you were part of some study that went awry."

"If I was, I certainly don't remember it," John frowned.

"It's true. Here, he gave me his card. He says if you contact him, he can help you." She slipped the card from her pocket and gave it to him.

John studied the card long and hard. "Why can't I remember any of this?"

"He thought you might not remember it. Apparently it was a very difficult time for you and, well…you broke beneath the pressure. Johnny has told me you needed an alter ego to face your frustrations with your police work. Once he emerged, you had a way to win against the criminal elements of the city without feeling guilty. Murdock has been using that to his advantage, giving Johnny assignments that have turned him into this vigilante."

John flushed angrily. "And he wants to help me? I highly doubt it. He probably wants to tinker with my head some more."

"That's what I thought at first too. But John, I think he's serious. The real deal. I think if anybody can begin to heal the breach in your two identities it's this man. We can't dismiss him out of turn."

"I can't trust him. If he did this to me then I can't trust him."

"I'll leave the decision up to you, but I think you should at least meet with him, to find out how you feel about him then."

John mulled over her words for a long moment. "I'll think about it," he said at last.

That was all Enya could have hoped for and she fell silent on the matter. "They've arrested two more Siren executives. They think the case might be able to go to court in as little time as a couple of months."

"That's good news. Maybe they'll back off from you now that it's clear the FBI has a strong case against them regardless."

"Maybe," she smiled.

John paused, his fork hovering before his mouth. "I love it when you smile," he said, his eyes alight like stars.

Enya blushed. She loved these soft times between them.

"Let's skip dinner and go to bed," he said wickedly.

"Why not just lay me out over this table," she teased.

She was unprepared when John cleared the table off, the dishes crashing to the floor.

"Don't do that, Argyle and Elliott might hear!"

"Let them hear. They know what we're up to in here." He practically jumped over the table to get to her. He lifted her from her chair, turned and bent her over the table. He pulled her pants down and ripped her panties off with a violent lust that left her shaken.

He freed his cock from his pants and rubbed it sensuously against her ass. His hands reached around her and plumped her breasts through the flimsy material of her T-shirt. The shirt hindered him from feeling her soft skin and he removed it with impatient hands.

Enya was eternally grateful that she hadn't worn a bra. Her nipples stabbed at his palms, hard and aching for his touch. John bit her softly at the nape of her neck, pushing her long dark hair over one shoulder to expose it. "I love the taste of your skin," he breathed.

Her knees turned to butter.

"But perhaps it needs something more," he said and left her, moving to the refrigerator. He emerged with a can of whipped cream.

Enya laughed. "Don't make me sticky," she protested.

"You'll be sticky either way once I'm done with you," he promised devilishly.

He came behind her and sprayed a line of the cream down her back. It was cold and she gasped, but the cold was soon replaced with the wild heat of his mouth as he licked away every last bit of cream.

"Mmmm, delicious," he said, and bent down behind her.

Enya was unprepared for what he did next. He sprayed whipped cream down the seam of her bottom. She thought to cry a protest, but when his mouth touched her, she went weak with ecstasy.

He licked her bottom, leaving no cream behind. When he was through Enya was shuddering, barely able to stand, even braced over the table as she was. John left her again, this time going for the bottle of hand lotion she kept near the sink.

This time she did protest.

"Shh," John told her cajolingly. "You'll like it, I promise."

He put a large dollop of cream between her cheeks, pressing some of the lotion into her anus. He moved his fingers in and out of her resisting flesh until she was soft and pliant beneath him. Then he rubbed some of the moisturizer onto his cock.

John pressed heavily into her, his cock beginning to stretch her ass. It was a long time, his hands roving over her body as if petting her, praising her for her acquiescence, but soon his cock head penetrated her opening.

Enya gasped at the intrusion but felt little pain. What pain she did feel only served to heighten her passion.

"Touch yourself," John said at her ear. "Touch your clit for me."

She shivered. But she did as he commanded, her fingers moving to her clit to slide and stroke in her own juices. Her body immediately loosened and John was able to slide deeper into her.

He had his hands on her hips, guiding her back against him even as he pressed inexorably closer. Enya cried out as he slid another inch inside of her.

"Shhh." He soothed her with his hands, cupping her breasts once more. Tweaking her nipples until she moaned and softened once again. He moved out of her and thrust back in, deeper.

Enya rubbed her clit and felt her body spasm around his cock. He gasped into her ear then groaned. "Do that again," he begged.

She clenched her muscles and smiled when he gasped again. She did it a third time and was astonished when he came with a long, harsh groan.

When he'd recovered, many moments later, he pulled his cock from her ass and turned her around to face him. "You have the most luscious ass I've ever seen," he said. "Thank you for that. Now it's your turn."

He laid her down on the table and put her legs around his neck. He bent his head to her pussy and began licking her like a cat licking at a bowl of cream. Now it was Enya who gasped and moaned.

He sucked her flesh into his mouth, his tongue stabbing into the heart of her.

She came with a shriek, the force of her release surprising her. She shuddered and quaked on the table, legs spread wide, pussy open to John's mouth. She came and came until her vision turned fuzzy. His mouth lapped at her all the while, taking her climax into his mouth.

When it was over Enya felt boneless, heavy and sleepy. She let John carry her to the bed, where she promptly fell asleep.

Chapter Twelve

ಬಿ

Noises from outside her apartment woke them hours later. It was still night, dark and dangerous. Enya shot up from the bed, gasping. John was much faster, rising to his feet with one long fluid movement that reminded her of Johnny.

"What was that?" she asked, stupefied.

"Gunshots," John said quietly. "Get dressed. Now."

Enya scrambled out of bed and grabbed the first items of clothing she could find—a worn pair of jeans and one of John's discarded shirts. Far too big, it swallowed her up, but she didn't mind or care. Wearing it immediately made her feel safer.

They ran to the sitting room and regarded the front door. "Should we open it?" she asked. "To see what's going on?"

"Be quiet," he said, listening. "Do you hear that?"

The door exploded as a missile tore through it.

"Holy fuck!" she screamed. "What was that?"

"Missile launcher. Damn it, they're really serious this time. Come on, we'll go out to the fire escape." He grabbed her arm and began to pull her to the window that would let them outside onto the ledge of the fire escape.

"What, are you crazy? That thing isn't nearly up to code— it'll collapse the minute we set foot on it."

"Well we can't get out the front," he growled, looking down at the three stories that separated them from the ground.

Enya looked out too, and they both watched as a red convertible drove beneath the escape.

"Jump!" Ryan Murdock called up to them in a shout.

Bullets tore into the apartment, shredding the walls. "Don't forget your briefcase — it has your gun in it!" Enya cried.

"Are we going to trust this guy?" he asked.

"It's Ryan Murdock, the man I told you about. He's not one of these assassins, believe me."

John nodded and left her, racing through the gunfire to get his briefcase. He grabbed it and returned. "I'll go first to make sure it's safe enough," he told her. He pressed a hard kiss against her mouth then pulled back, his eyes stunned. Enya had no time to ask him what was wrong. John stepped out and the metal of the fire stairs groaned a loud protest. He jumped into the backseat of the car below.

"Come on baby doll, I'll catch you," he called.

Enya stepped out onto the fire escape, which dipped alarmingly. She heard voices from inside her apartment and knew she couldn't waste another second. She closed her eyes and jumped. She landed with a hard, jarring thud onto the seat and John's arms closed around her. As Ryan peeled rubber, Enya looked back to see the fire escape collapse to the ground in a shower of metal and rust.

"Oh God, that was close," she panted.

Ryan sped the car through the dark night.

"How did you know to come for us, Ryan?" Enya asked.

"I've had one man or another watching your apartment for the last week, keeping an eye out for Johnny. I was on watch tonight when I heard the explosion. Lucky thing, too, because none of my men have convertibles."

Enya laughed hysterically and realized she must be going into shock. John held her tighter to him, soothing her with his hands, and she quieted.

"Pull over," John said suddenly.

"Why?" Ryan shot back over his shoulder.

"Because I want to drive. I want to know where we're going."

"I can take you back to Sterling."

"No," John said firmly. "We'll go downtown to the precinct."

"Do you really think, after all this effort, that a few policemen will dissuade Siren from trying to kill her again?"

John subsided somewhat. But he held firm to his resolve. "Let me drive," he said.

Ryan pulled the car over into a deserted alleyway. He and John got out of the car and faced each other.

"I know you," John said, frowning.

"Yes," Ryan nodded. "You've known me well for awhile now."

"I don't remember how we met," he said.

"I'm not surprised by that, John."

"Why are you here? Why now? Can't you see this situation is complicated enough without you interfering and meddling with my life?" John demanded.

"I only want to help you, Johnny."

"Don't you fucking call me that!" John roared.

Ryan disappeared with a loud popping noise then reappeared behind John. John whirled around to face him again, an incredulous look on his face. "How the bloody hell did you do that?"

"We're a lot alike, you and I. We are human, but so much more."

"What are you talking about?"

"I'm talking about your unique abilities. Your gifts. Your ability to see time slow to a crawl so that you can chase through it. But where you bend time and space to move at your preternatural speed, I don't move at all. I can simply will myself anywhere I wish to go."

"This is too bizarre," John said hoarsely. "I can't believe this is happening."

"Tell me about it," Ryan laughed. "I deal with these sorts of things every day."

"I can't believe in all this." John ran his hands through his hair.

"Let me take you to Sterling. You'll be safe there, both of you, I give you my word. I can help you, John. I can help you to become whole again."

John appeared to capitulate when two cars pulled up, one in front of the convertible, one at the back, effectively penning them in.

"Oh shit," Enya breathed, as one of the cars' doors opened and a hulking brute of a man stepped out holding a machine gun in his hands. "John, I think it's time to put your hat on," she said in a weak voice.

John reached for the briefcase, opening it so fast not even the hit man pointing the gun at her could follow his movements. He pulled out his hat and guns then turned to fire at their assailant.

All the car doors opened now and men got out of both to shoot at Johnny, who easily danced between the bullets. Johnny hit two of the men, bringing them down easily.

A man came up behind Enya and she screamed, kicking out at him when he tried to grab her. Johnny turned and fired one of his enormous hand cannons, hitting the man in the shoulder. She crawled out of the car, bullets whizzing by her ear, and tried to make it to Johnny's side.

A gun pressed to her head and she stilled.

"You've been an awful lot of trouble to us. But you can't dodge a bullet like your man can." He squeezed the trigger.

And something pushed her out of the way a millionth of a second before the gun fired. Johnny had used his speed to reach her, shoving her out of harm's way.

Johnny fell, a large red stain blooming on his chest.

The alleyway flooded with light as several unmarked cars pulled up. Men got out of the cars and pointed their guns at Enya's remaining attackers. "Freeze or we'll open fire," someone shouted.

Still more cars pulled up. The newcomers, she assumed, were the police.

Everything happened so fast, Enya's head spun. As the police and government agents swarmed in to handcuff her attackers, she went to her knees on the ground by Johnny's side.

"Don't die," she said cradling him to her. "Hold on. Don't die."

Ryan was at her side. "My men here will take him. We'll save him, don't worry," he promised.

"These are your men?" she asked, dazed. She'd thought the unmarked cars meant the FBI had arrived.

"Yes. They'll take care of you both, I swear it."

Johnny groaned and spat out a mouthful of blood. "Go with them, Enya. They'll keep you safe." He coughed again, the sound wet and deep.

"Oh John, hang on, don't let go. Don't let go of me," she chanted like a mantra. "I'm here. I love you."

"Oh baby doll, I love you too," he answered, using the name John Spada always called her.

Was he Johnny Vicious now, as he lay dying, or was he John Spada? Enya couldn't tell.

"When I kissed you, the earth moved for me. I remembered all the times I'd kissed you as Vicious. I don't know how but your kiss has healed a part of me." He spat out a mouthful of blood.

"Don't talk like this."

"I have to. Might not have another chance." He coughed again. "God, I wish I'd met you sooner so we'd have had more time together."

Enya cried out as he spasmed in her arms. "Hang on. Just hang on. *Please* baby, just hang on…"

Chapter Thirteen
Three months later

೫

Siren has officially filed for bankruptcy after five of their operating staff were indicted on Tuesday for money laundering, tax evasion, illegal genetic research and attempted murder…

Enya turned off the television and sat in silence for a long while. It was finally over. All of it. The bastards who ran Siren were behind bars where they belonged. Her testimony had seen to that. As had Argyle's and Elliott's, for they had been witnesses and victims to the attack on her apartment. Along with the FBI's damning evidence, which they had been collecting for almost a decade, there was no amount of money that could save the corporation. Enya was safe. Here, in Sterling, Siren could never touch her again.

John came and sat next to her on the couch, wincing as he did, for his chest was still a little tender even after three months of healing. "Nothing good on TV?" he asked.

"No." She smiled at him.

"Have I told you today how much I love you?" he asked.

Her smile broadened. "No."

"How about I show you then," he said, and leaned her back onto the couch, covering her with his body.

"Don't you have a meeting with Ryan soon, in therapy?"

"In half an hour," he grumbled. He hated his therapy sessions, but they were doing him some good. Ryan had been as good as his word, helping John to fuse his two personalities together with gentle and experienced patience.

More and more often John seemed whole again. A fusion of both personalities that never failed to keep Enya on her toes.

"But that should be long enough for a quickie," he cajoled, grinning devilishly at her, his light green eyes bright with desire.

Within seconds they had their clothes off and were completely nude and wrapped in each other's embrace.

John positioned her on top of him and she sank down over his cock slowly. Her body was wet and hot for him, as it always was. Her nipples hot and hard as his fingers played with them.

Her hair fell across his face, tickling him as she began to rock on top of him.

"You're so beautiful," he breathed, pulling her head down to kiss her thoroughly.

Enya melted further onto him. Into him. His arms came around her, holding her tight. He bucked his hips up into hers, filling her deeper with this thick, wide cock. She cried out, letting him bounce her on him, her breasts bobbing down so that he could take her nipples with his mouth.

His hands wandered down to her bottom, spreading her cheeks wide. His finger traced the ridge of her anus and Enya spasmed around his cock. They both moaned raggedly. He thrust in and out of her body, over and over again, the wet sounds their bodies made reaching their ears.

Enya came first, crying out, clutching him to her. John soon followed, filling her with his cream—hot and wild into her quivering body.

She collapsed down onto him. "I love you," she gasped, out of breath.

"I love you too, baby doll," he said and held her tight.

Epilogue

ॐ

John looked at his briefcase, the combination set to 777. He opened it and took out his guns, coat and hat.

He remembered more and more, the things Johnny had done. He regretted nothing, seeing the nobility in what he and Sterling had accomplished. John had even begun to learn how to use his preternatural speed, his Time Chasing as Ryan Murdock called it. It seemed that Johnny was gone, melding with him so completely that John couldn't distinguish between the two anymore.

But he wondered…

He put the hat on.

Lightning thundered outside. And everything went black…

Enya came up behind him and put her arms around him. "Don't worry John, that was just the power going out because of the storm."

"I know. And call me Johnny."

Fyre

ॐ

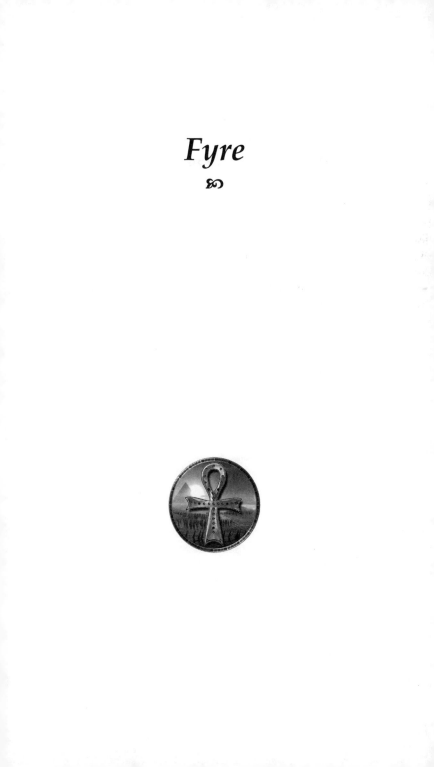

Trademarks Acknowledgement

~

The author acknowledges the trademarked status and trademark owners of the following wordmarks mentioned in this work of fiction:

Beretta: Fabbrica D'armi P. Beretta, S.P.A. Corporation

Expedition: Ford Motor Company

Prologue
ഇ

Ryan Murdock watched as the woman he loved was hooked up to an EKG machine. This wasn't the first time she'd been at Sterling headquarters. She'd been coming here since she turned twelve years old. And Ryan had been with her every time, though she may not have known it.

Ryan had fallen in love with Mia upon first seeing her here on that long ago day. He'd been eighteen at the time, but he'd known that she was the one for him. Now she was a woman grown, twenty-six years old to his thirty-two, and she still had no idea of his feelings for her.

The scientists at Sterling had yet to understand exactly how Mia's powers worked, but they had catalogued and studied her case extensively and they had helped her to control her violent outbursts over the years.

Mia was a fire starter. A pyrokenetic. A very rare and very volatile breed indeed.

It had been many months since Mia's last visit to the Sterling compound, and Ryan felt that she had never looked more beautiful than she did now. Oh, how he coveted her. He wanted nothing more than to sink his face into her long blonde hair and breathe deeply of her unique scent. But now was not the time. It was never the right time.

Mia had had an accident. It was why she was here. She had been working at the aquarium when it happened — a burst of fiery energy that had shattered over a dozen tanks and sent onlookers running away in terror. It had been two years since her last accident. Mia was devastated that it had happened again. She'd thought — as had the scientists at Sterling — that her attacks were over for good. How wrong they had been.

After a few tests to prove her health was in good condition she would be free to go. Ryan had no idea when or if he'd see her again. It tore him apart inside every time she left Sterling, but he watched her go rather than tell her his feelings. He couldn't bear the thought of her rejection, and he dared not chance it.

Mia wasn't too fond of him, he was certain. It was understandable. She associated him with her accidents, for she only saw him at Sterling and she usually only came to Sterling when there was a problem with her powers. Much as he might have wanted to, Ryan couldn't change that fact.

She looked so fragile there beneath the electrodes and among all the medical equipment. Ryan, standing behind a two-way mirror, watched as she bravely sat still under her doctors' ministrations and he couldn't help but admire her bravery.

He himself hated being poked and prodded by doctors, scientists or their like. He never had been able to sit still as Mia now did. It was a good thing his own powers were easily controlled or else he would have found himself a subject of study for the Sterling scientists more often.

Mia sat up on the table, affording Ryan a peek at her sleekly rounded shoulder beneath the paper dress she wore. She got down from the table carefully as those around her tidied up, and approached the mirror.

Ryan instinctively took a step back, even knowing that she couldn't possibly see him through the mirror. She put a hand up over her eyes and leaned in against the glass. Ryan felt the weight of her gaze as though she were standing there in the room with him.

Mia smiled and Ryan's heart beat a thunderous tattoo in his chest. Could she see him after all?

One of the doctors caught Mia's attention and she turned away from the mirror. Ryan breathed a heavy sigh of relief— then watched with renewed interest as she embraced a male doctor.

Jealousy, fast and hot, took him in a rush. He clenched his fists in rage as Mia pulled back to place a kiss on the man's cheek. Mark was the doctor's name. Ryan remembered it now and vowed retribution swift and sure. He gritted his teeth until they hurt and watched as the two parted once more.

Mia gathered her clothes and went into the adjoining bathroom to change. Ryan turned to leave the secret observation room, determined to find out just what was between the doctor and his patient. He made his way around to the room Mia had vacated.

Mark Longbottom started when he saw Ryan enter the room.

Ryan wasted no time. "Are you and Mia seeing each other now?"

Mark frowned. "No, of course not. Why do you ask?"

Ryan pointed to the two-way mirror. "I saw you hugging. And kissing," he accused.

Mark shook his head. "Relax, Ryan. We're just friends."

Ryan felt his fists unclench by small degrees. "How is she?" he asked, changing the subject.

"She's fine. A little shaken, but that's to be expected."

"Do you have any idea what might have triggered this attack?"

Mark sighed. "Unfortunately, no. We've never been able to pinpoint exactly how or why her abilities manifest themselves. It might have been stress. It might have been something she changed in her diet. We just don't know."

Mia came out of the bathroom fully dressed. "Hello, Ryan," she said softly.

"Hello, Mia. Are you all right?"

Mia's dewy lips trembled and she pursed them. "I'm fine." Her perfectly violet gaze grew hooded and guarded.

"I've already spoken to the aquarium. Sterling paid for the damages and your employers have been apprised of your situation, though I doubt they believed it. However, they are willing to allow you back at work as soon as you're ready. You've a good reputation there. And since the damages are paid for, they won't seek legal action against you."

Mia shook her head. "I can't go back there now. It might happen again. I can't chance that."

"What will you do?"

Mia sighed. "I'll look for another job I guess."

Ryan took a deep breath. "You could always stay here and work with us."

"And be one of your so-called vigilantes? No thanks, Ryan. I'd rather take my own chances out in the real world. I'd like *some* semblance of normalcy in my life."

"But Mia, you're not normal." He could have kicked himself the moment the words left his mouth. "Stay here with us, with other people like you. We understand you here. We can help you cope."

"No, Ryan. I tried living here for ten years and it didn't work. I'll always be an anomaly, even here at Sterling. Let it go."

Ryan pursed his lips and subsided. "Will you at least stay here tonight? So I can be sure you're safe."

Mia smiled and Ryan's heart tripped into double time. "Sure Ryan. I'd like that I think."

"Your apartment is just as you left it the last time you stayed with us."

"Thanks Ryan, you're sweet."

Ryan almost scowled. He didn't want her to think him *sweet*, damn it. "Thanks," he muttered.

Ryan resolved to prove to her, before her stay was over, that he was far, far from sweet.

Chapter One

ନ୍ତ

Mia Fyre stepped into her Sterling apartment and closed the door quietly behind her. She rested against it heavily with a deeply felt sigh.

Ryan was more handsome now than ever. His hair, blond and shining, was getting long around his neck. It gave him a rakish air. All he needed to complete the look was a gold ring in his ear. His dark blue eyes had seemed to see right through her calm façade. Her heart had tripped upon seeing him there in the observation room with Mark.

She hadn't been prepared to see Ryan. She was never prepared to see him.

She'd been attracted to Ryan since she was fifteen years old. He'd been twenty-one at the time and training to fill his father's shoes. He'd seemed a knight in shining armor to her then. She'd relished every moment they had spent in each other's company. She knew he had no idea of her feelings—in fact she'd gone to great lengths to make sure that he didn't.

Mia didn't need this complication on top of her troubles. She would have preferred not to see Ryan at all, to simply get her tests over with and leave Sterling undetected, but he'd surprised her. He always seemed to be around when she came to Sterling. It was most unsettling.

An image of exploding aquarium tanks flooded her mind and she moaned. She'd thought she was free of these accidents forever. Now she knew that was far, far from the truth. This accident had been the worst yet. People had witnessed it, and even if they didn't quite understand what they had seen, they all knew she was the cause of it.

Pity. She had really liked her job at the aquarium.

Someone knocked on the door and she jumped with a tiny, surprised cry. She shook herself and opened the door.

Mia felt her eyes grow wide. "What are you doing here Ryan?" she asked, as he pushed his way into the apartment and glanced around.

"I wanted to know if you needed any food or supplies."

"I'm only going to be staying here tonight. I can forage in the cupboards just fine."

"It's been awhile since you were here last. Don't you want something fresh to eat?"

She blew a stray lock of hair out of her face. "Canned food doesn't go bad for a long time."

Ryan nodded and sat down on her sofa as if he planned on staying awhile. Mia steeled her nerves to handle his nearness, desperately hoping that he couldn't see how much she wanted him.

"We want you back at Sterling," he said softly.

Mia sat on a chair opposite the couch. His words made her heart skip a beat. "I know. But I just can't stay here. This place is…well, it's so far apart from a normal life. And all I've ever wanted is a normal life out there in the big world."

"You can lead a normal life here."

"And watch as patient after patient moves through these walls? No thank you. I've had enough of strange people to last me a lifetime."

"They aren't strange. Just gifted. Like you."

"I'm not gifted," she gritted out, "I'm cursed."

Ryan eyed her with those startling, intense blue eyes. "You didn't always feel cursed."

Mia shook her head. "That was so long ago. We were still just kids."

"You've never been a kid, Mia," Ryan pointed out.

And she hadn't. From the first accident she'd been more than a kid. She'd grown up in a short space of time, and it had been a complete change. Just as everything else in her life had gone up in flames, so too had her childhood.

Being watched so closely beneath that blue gaze made her palms sweat and she fidgeted in her seat. Ryan saw too much, knew too much, especially about her. He looked at her now as if he could see into the heart of her — know all her secrets, uncover all her shame.

"Ryan, I don't want to go through this tonight. I just want to rest and try to forget the day."

"You can't just wipe the slate clean, you know. How many times have you had to start your life over out there in the real world? It hasn't worked before, so why do you insist on trying again?"

Mia, frustrated, ran a hand through her hair. "I'll try a million more times if I have to, until I get it right. And I *will* get it right, eventually. I must."

"The outside world is no place for people like you and I. We need a safe place, a home. Here at Sterling you can have that. Stay here where it's safe."

"Ryan, I've never been safe. And by staying here I put your staff, your friends at risk. Don't you remember what happened — "

"Don't bring that up again. That was an accident, Mia, it could have happened anywhere, at any time."

"I firebombed the lab where they were working with Steele. If it hadn't been for Steele's thick skin, I would have burned him pretty badly. Perhaps even killed him," she pointed out.

"But his skin *is* thick and you didn't hurt him at all."

"I know, but what about the next time? Can you promise me that I won't hurt anyone next time? I don't think you can," she sighed.

"I'll put some of the new doctors on your team. They'll help you find a cure," Ryan persisted.

"There is no cure for what I am—only death can make this horrible power go away."

"Don't you dare say such things!" he roared. "Don't even think them!" He sobered slightly. "Look, you've got nothing better to do, why not try it again here with us?"

"Why do you keep insisting that I stay here?" she asked.

"Because you belong here."

"I don't belong anywhere," she said flatly.

"You belong *here*."

Mia closed her eyes—it was the only way she could hide from that intense stare of his. "Maybe I'll try."

"Don't try. Just do it," he said.

She sighed heavily. "Oh all right. I'll stay here. But only," she held her hand up when Ryan would have spoken, "for a couple of days. Until I find a new job."

Ryan nodded. "That'll give me time to convince you to stay for good."

Mia laughed. "You're not making it easier for me to stay here at all."

"Life is never easy. You know that."

Mia sobered. "I know. But I sometimes like to pretend that it is."

"Don't we all?" Ryan stood up, came forward and pressed a soft, brotherly kiss on her forehead, making her heart skip a beat at his nearness. He tucked an errant lock of hair back behind her ear, winked down at her, then left her there in the room.

It was a long, long time before her pulse beat slowed back to normal and her erratic breathing slowed.

Chapter Two
Two days later

જી

Ryan was having a helluva time staying away from Mia. He was afraid to spend too much time with her, afraid of what he might do. Afraid that she might see just how much he wanted her.

She seemed so fragile now, as if this latest accident had sapped her of all her strength and will. Her skin, already delicate and pale, was even more so now. Her beautiful violet eyes had dark circles beneath them and she hardly ate anything that Ryan sent to her room. More than once in the past two days he'd caught sight of her and had to keep himself under an iron control to avoid scaring her away.

Mia spent her days in the lab, letting the scientists study her as best they could in the hopes that this time, at last, they would discover the secret to unlocking her powers. Ryan often made it a point to stop by the lab, just to look in on her and secretly ask the technicians how she was progressing under their care.

At night, Mia never seemed to sleep. Ryan's home was only two doors down from hers and he often found himself walking by her apartment to see if there was any light shining through below the door. There always was. And from the muffled noises coming from inside the apartment, Ryan knew that Mia wasn't sleeping with the lights on. She was pacing.

Ryan wished there was something he could do to help her overcome this latest setback. But every time he got close to her, close enough to offer comfort, he found himself wanting to give her comfort of another sort entirely. He didn't want to push her anymore than he already had. But it was harder each time to turn away from her.

Mia was all he could think about anymore. He couldn't concentrate on his work, he couldn't eat or sleep or dream without thinking of her. Before, he'd been able to block thoughts of her from his mind simply by immersing himself in work. But this time his fascination was so strong that he couldn't redirect his thoughts no matter how hard he tried.

Maybe it was because his two best men, Steele and Vicious, were married now. Ryan saw their happiness every day shining bright on their faces and on the faces of their wives. Love was in the air at Sterling. It was driving him daft, and all because he couldn't have the object of his own desire. Mia was her own person—she'd never let an overbearing, stubborn, arrogant brute like Ryan be a part of her life, and he well knew it. Wedded bliss, it seemed, was too far beyond his reach.

Ryan snapped a pencil in his hand and looked down at the broken fragments of wood lying in his palm. This was how his heart felt every time he saw Mia. Splintered. He wondered why he didn't just let her go back out into the world. After all, she didn't want to stay at Sterling. But no matter how rational it sounded, he simply couldn't seem to let her go. Not this time.

There had to be an opportune moment to tell Mia just how he felt about her. But if there had been so far, Ryan hadn't seen it. The only time he ever saw her anymore was when she was having a hard go of it. While she was weak, while she was so fragile she looked as if she might break, he couldn't open his heart to her.

But why? Mia was a big girl. Independent to a fault and stubborn as a mule besides, she could take care of herself. Why shouldn't he confront her, tell her what was on his mind and in his heart? More than once Mia had pointed out to him that she was no longer a child. Perhaps it was time he stopped treating her like one and appealed to the woman he knew was inside her.

Ryan rose from behind his desk. He grabbed a piece of peppermint from the candy dish on his desk and popped it into his mouth. Peppermints had always been his favorite candy. He was heading for the door when, unexpectedly, it opened.

"I need to speak with you, Ryan," Steele said.

Ryan motioned for the large, muscular man to sit in a seat opposite his. "What's on your mind, Steele?"

"I've just received information that, to save themselves from bankruptcy, Siren is about to go public with their cerebral enhancing chips."

"No one will believe them. And even if they did, do you think people will willingly allow chips to be glued to their heads? I think not."

"Siren isn't marketing them as a mind-control device. They're appealing to the techno geeks and computer nerds by calling it an 'electronic enhancement' device. They're going to claim that it's safe and that it boosts brain power."

"God, nothing could be further from the truth." Ryan swore colorfully.

"What should we do about it?" Steele asked.

"Well, we can't let them market this product to the public. It would go against every principle that Sterling stands for." Ryan rubbed a hand over his face in frustration. "What do they hope to gain by doing this? The public simply isn't ready for this kind of technology. I'm not sure anyone will ever be ready for it."

"My sentiments exactly. But how do we stop them?"

Ryan took a deep breath. "Call Vicious for a meeting. We'll try to figure this out together."

"Vicious and Enya went out for the night. It'll have to wait until morning."

Ryan started. "It's already night? I thought it was no later than afternoon."

Steele chuckled. "You work too hard, Ryan. You've been cooped up here all day. You need to take a break from all this."

"I don't have time to take a break. Especially not now that Siren is making a move on the public market."

"I hear that Mia is back," Steele said pointedly.

"She is," Ryan growled.

"I might swing by her apartment and visit with her for awhile," Steele said with a sly smile.

Ryan gritted his teeth hard. "You're a married man now, Steele. She's off limits to you."

Steele laughed outright at that. "You always were the jealous type. I only have to mention her name and you're on me like a rottweiler. Why don't you just tell her how you feel?"

"I'll tell her how I feel in due time. Stop trying to rile me."

Steele shrugged. "Well, don't wait forever Ryan, or you might lose her."

"I won't." Ryan rose once more and headed for the door. "I'll see you in the morning, Steele." He motioned for the giant man to leave.

Steele stepped through the door. "Bye boss." He saluted jauntily and strode off in the direction of the apartment he shared with Marla, deep within the Sterling compound. Ryan watched him go with something that felt like relief. Steele saw too much that Ryan wanted to keep hidden. Steele had always been like that, ever since Ryan's father, William Murdock, had taken the lonely, beaten boy under his wing.

Ryan felt his resolve harden. He would tell Mia how he felt. But he'd do it his own way. And hope that Mia didn't turn away from him in scorn.

* * * * *

Mia sank down low into the warm bubble bath. The extra large garden tub in her bathroom was probably the thing she missed most about living at Sterling. It was pure heaven to submerge herself in the hot water and let all of the day's worries wash down the drain.

She'd received the results of all her tests just before retiring for the night. And as she'd suspected they might, the tests revealed nothing about why or how she'd had her accident.

Technology, it seemed, just hadn't caught up to a pyrokenetic's abilities quite yet. Mia wondered if it ever would.

With a determined purse of her lips, Mia raised one hand from the water and held it up before her face. She gave a push with her mind and willed the fire that burned so brightly inside of her, even now, to spring forth.

Her hand jerked and then was consumed in a pure violet flame that licked its way up her arm. Mia felt its heat but did not feel any pain from it. She turned her hand this way and that, watching the flames as they grew bigger and bigger. The flames started licking around the ends of her hair and she squeezed her eyes shut at the brightness of them.

Before the flames could get out of control, she submerged her hand in the bubbly water. The flames sputtered but did not go out, even under the liquid. They did, however, heat her bath up rather quickly. Mia gave another push with her mind, imagining a brick wall slamming down on that part of her brain that controlled the fire. Or controlled it as much as possible.

The fire flickered then went out. Mia raised her hand before her face again, looking for injuries, redness, anything that would provide proof of what she'd just done. But there was nothing. There never was. The skin of this hand looked as clean and healthy as it did on the other hand. There were no burns, no blisters, nothing. Mia sighed heavily and leaned back in the tub once more.

She rubbed a sponge over her breasts and belly, soaping herself up until she was slippery and white with suds and bubbles. Her nipples stabbed into the cold air and her breasts floated on the surface of the water like two large melons. Mia looked down at her body, past her breasts to her belly and beyond, and frowned. She could stand to lose ten or twenty pounds, that much was for certain.

Not that it really mattered. She wasn't in the market for a lover. And even if she had been it shouldn't matter what she looked like. She was healthy. She was strong. That was enough for her to be happy. Any man interested in her should feel the same way.

But Mia wasn't stupid. She knew how the world worked. How men wanted nothing less than perfection in their women. Damn men, anyway. What did they know about beauty? They were too busy starting wars and committing crimes to know what true beauty was.

Mia could have kicked herself for her negative thoughts. Not all men were war-hungry criminals. Just a large portion of them.

She laughed at that thought and dunked her head under the warm water. She held her breath as long as she could, turning her head this way and that to get every strand of her hair wet, then resurfaced.

She shrieked when she saw Ryan standing in the doorway.

"What the hell are you doing here?" she demanded, sloshing water over the rim of the tub.

Ryan's eyes roved over her and she was thankful that the suds covered most of her body. She sank lower to be sure her breasts were covered as well.

"I knocked several times and you didn't answer. I thought maybe you'd slipped out to go back home," he said.

Mia pursed her lips. "Well, now you know I'm here. Please leave, Ryan."

Ryan walked into the room.

"Ryan! Leave. I'm taking a bath here," she pointed out unnecessarily.

But Ryan did not turn to leave. Instead he came even farther into the bathroom, stalking forward like an overgrown jungle cat, until the tips of his shoes touched the side of the tub.

Mia crossed her arms over her breasts protectively. "What's wrong with you, Ryan?"

"What's wrong?" Ryan let out a long, slow breath. "I'll tell you what's wrong. That you're in that tub without me. That'll work for starters."

Mia shrieked again as he stepped into the tub, shoes and clothes and all, and bent down to straddle her legs, his knees on either side of her thighs in the water. "What are you doing?"

"Something I've wanted to do for years," Ryan said, and bent his head to hers. He pressed his lips first to her forehead, then to her nose, then—oh then!—he laid his lips upon hers.

Mia's eyes went wide as he moved his mouth over hers. She felt his tongue stroke over her bottom lip and gasped, allowing him full access to her. He ravaged her mouth, pressing harder until their teeth clicked together. His tongue slid past her lips and tangled with hers, delving deep. Mia's eyes closed and the moment swept her up on a tidal wave of too-long-denied need.

Ryan put his warm, wet hands on either side of her face, trapping her in his kiss. The spicy, manly smell of him permeated her nostrils. The delicate, sweet flavor of him filled her mouth. He'd been eating peppermints—Mia remembered now that they were his favorite candy. Mia shivered as his hands lowered and came around to press in the small of her back.

He lifted her lightly, easily, bringing her body out of the water and into his arms. The scratchy linen of his shirt scraped her sensitive nipples. The rough corduroy of his pants pressed into her belly, against the mound of her sex, making her feel both vulnerable and powerful at the same time.

With easy strength he turned her in the tub until she lay gently back over the side of it, so that her breasts were high and exposed to him. His mouth burned a path down her jaw, to her throat and then her chest. His hands steadied her and his mouth slurped in one of her nipples, making her cry out and moan. His teeth came into play, scraping over her tender flesh lightly as he sucked her into his wet, hot mouth.

His hands roamed over her, petting her, teasing her. He ran his hand over her breast, plumping and squeezing it until she burned. His other hand stroked down over her midriff and stomach, teasing her as his touch wandered below the water.

The touch of his fingers in her slit sent a bolt of electricity shooting through her and she cried out her surprise. He held her fast when she would have pulled away and cupped her fully in his palm, rubbing her erotically. Her nipple popped free and his mouth caught her cries as he found and stroked her swollen, needy clit.

Mia arched up beneath him, opening her mouth wider to his demanding kiss, sucking his tongue when he would let her, stroking hers inside his mouth when he wouldn't. She brought her legs up and around his waist, allowing him easier access to her aching, throbbing pussy.

His finger stroked her deep. His hand found her pleasure hole and he slipped two large, long fingers into the heart of her need. Mia moaned, feeling his questing fingers slip in her body's moisture, sensation sweeping her from head to toe.

Mia shivered. Ryan suckled her full lower lip into his mouth. His fingers curved inside her body—thrusting so deep she felt the touch reverberate inside her womb. His hair tickled her face like a thousand roaming, caressing fingers. His lips were the softest she'd ever kissed, his flavor and scent wildly intoxicating like nothing she'd ever before experienced…

Ryan pulled back with a gasp, his lips and hands leaving her suddenly bereft. He watched her from behind heavily lidded eyes. Mia fought the urge to cover herself again—it was a little too late for modesty. Even she knew that. His eyes roved over her from head to toe, lingering on her breasts and cunt. Mia felt her face blush and looked away.

"I'm sorry," Ryan said softly, shakily, realizing he must have scared her with his ardor—even if she seemed to be hiding it well. He rose from the bath, his clothes soaked and dripping on the floor. "I couldn't help myself."

"Don't apologize." Her voice sounded hoarse even to her own ears.

"I'm not sorry that I did it. Only that I shocked you," he clarified, blue gaze burning through her. "I should have gone slower."

Ryan turned and left her there, speechless. He disappeared in the blink of an eye, the loud popping noise of his teleportation echoing about the room. She put her hands to her lips and felt his touch there still. Tasted him. Smelled him. Her body remembered the touch of his hands, her nipples hard and aching, her pussy wet and throbbing with desire.

What was she going to do now? Where did she go from here? She didn't know the answers to those questions and it frightened her.

All she did know was that she wanted Ryan to touch her, to kiss her again. She rose from the bath and went to get a robe, determined that before the evening was out, she would be in Ryan's arms again.

Chapter Three

๛

Ryan cursed himself for being a thousand fools. He'd frightened her—of that much he was certain. Shocked and appalled her no doubt. Damn his wild need for her! Now Mia would probably never let him get close to her again.

He'd acted like a beast. Like a rogue. Taken advantage of her nudity, her vulnerability and her tender feelings. He hated himself for what he'd done in a moment of utter weakness. Why hadn't he simply turned away once he'd seen her in the bath and known she was all right, that she was still at Sterling, that she hadn't left him again?

He could have kicked himself. He wanted to. And yet a part of him was wickedly satisfied that he'd done what he'd done.

She'd been wet and slippery around his thrusting fingers. She'd wanted him, or at least her body had.

Pacing the floor of his apartment over and over, he racked his brain for a solution to this new problem. He had to find a way to make her forgive him for his trespass. He had to earn her trust once more, if it killed him. But how? It was plain for anyone to see that he wanted Mia. How could he convince her that such a thing wouldn't happen again when he wanted nothing *more* than to do it again and again and again?

There came a soft knock at his door. Ryan frowned, wondering who it could be, and opened the door. He was in no mood for visitors.

He felt his jaw drop open in surprise at seeing Mia standing there in her robe, waiting for him to answer her knock. She strode in without so much as an invitation, shouldering her way past him when he wouldn't move out of the way to let her pass.

Mia looked at him, letting her eyes drink in the sight of him from head to toe and back. He was still dressed in his soaking wet clothes, his hair disheveled from running his hand through it too many times.

"You ran away before I could speak to you," she said.

Ryan closed the door and leaned back heavily against it. "What is it?" He tried and failed not to sound gruff and abrupt.

"You left me in a state," she said.

Ryan ran a hand over his face. He smelled her scent on his fingers and moaned silently. "I'm sorry. I didn't mean for it to go so far."

"Do you mean that?" she asked, tilting her head to one side so that her wet, long blonde hair spilled down to her elbows.

Ryan looked into her mysterious violet eyes and found he could not lie to her, not now. "No. I wanted it to go further," he admitted hoarsely. "But not without your permission."

Mia seemed to think his words over for a minute. Then her hands went to the belt of her robe and undid the knot. She let the robe fall uselessly to the floor, standing there before him in all her nude glory, shameless and unafraid. "Is this permission enough for you?"

Ryan could have choked on his ragged breathing, so surprised was he at this unexpected turn of events. He couldn't look away from her beautiful, sexy body. Her nipples, long and pink, sat high atop her pert breasts. The rounded swell of her stomach softened her look, and her long, long legs stood strong and straight and proud.

Where was the fragile woman he'd always thought her to be?

Mia stalked him, coming closer, until the tips of her toes touched the tips of his shoes. "I said, is this permission enough for you?" She leaned in close to him.

Ryan's hands shook so badly he didn't know if he could put them on her without scaring her. He gritted his teeth and steeled himself. He felt Mia take his hands and place them atop her breasts. He groaned and leaned into her.

Her nipples stabbed hard into his palms, like tiny pebbles. Mia took a deep breath, her chest rising high beneath his touch. She put her hands on the buttons of his shirt, making short work of undoing them, and pushed it back to reveal his broad, muscular shoulders.

Ryan took her in his arms and pressed her naked chest to his. He bent his head to hers, slowly, to give her time to pull away should she choose to, and laid his lips upon hers. His hands splayed wide over her back and buttocks, pressing her deeper into his embrace so that every evidence of his arousal was undeniable.

With a feral growl he swept her up into his arms, his lips never leaving hers. He carried her from the living room into his darkened bedroom. He flicked the light switch on and laid her down upon the tall, king-sized bed. There came a popping noise—the noise of his teleportation—and in a blink he was completely nude.

Mia drank in the sight of him. He was so tall, so long of limb, but muscular more than lean. He had a wide torso that dipped into a small waist. His legs were endlessly long and thick with roped muscle. His body was hairless but for a light trail of fur that led down to the blond thatch of hair surrounding his cock.

And his cock! It was enormous. Thick as her wrist and long—at least nine inches, probably more—it bobbed toward her like a dousing rod. Mia reached for it, cupping it lovingly in her palms. Ryan let out a harsh expulsion of air and grabbed her hands. He didn't immediately pull them away, and Mia was afforded the opportunity to pump him not once but three times before he finally broke free of her grasp.

"Slow down," he whispered, pressing wicked little kisses to her ears and throat.

But Mia had waited too long for this moment. "No. Go faster," she demanded. "I can't wait for this, you devil," she gasped.

Ryan's lips wandered down her throat to her collarbone and beyond to her breasts. He slurped one nipple into his mouth, using his teeth on her until her nipple poked long and hard into his kiss. He visited the same upon her other breast, his wet sucking sounds filling both their ears and increasing their ardor.

His hands roamed down her body with a masterful knowledge that sent her head to spinning. The tips of his fingers trailed down her body from her throat to her knees, missing nothing in between. He tugged at her nipples, stroked the swell of her stomach, and delved teasingly between her legs before petting her thighs and spreading them wider.

Mia gasped and put her hands in his hair. She held on tight as he kissed his way down her body, knowing what he meant to do. Fearing and anticipating it at the same time.

The first touch of his tongue on her slit made her cry out a harsh sound of surprise and ecstasy. When his fingers spread her wide for his mouth she bucked, bringing his face even closer against her. His lips found her clit and he suckled it much the same as he had suckled her breasts. He tongued her, flicking over her most sensitive flesh until she was mindlessly tugging on his hair in her overwhelming passion.

He kissed his way back up her body and settled himself between her legs. She wrapped them around him, locking her ankles behind his back, and rubbed her wet, aching pussy against the hard ridge of his cock.

Ryan gasped and positioned himself at her opening. He caught her gaze with his. "Watch me."

Mia looked down and watched as Ryan took his cock in his hand and rubbed it up and down her slit. He slipped into the valley where her pleasure hole waited, empty and bereft without him. He pressed up into her, deeply, the thick, round head of him popping her cherry with hardly any pain.

He slid home, going balls deep inside of her. Stretching her impossibly around the thick impalement of his cock. Mia felt two tears slide down her temples and held him tight against her lest he see them. Ryan groaned long and loud, his weight settling heavier against her.

The muscles of his buttocks flexed and he began thrusting in and out of her, gently and then by degrees, harder and harder. Each impalement of his body within hers made her cry out, but in rising passion, not pain. She could feel him so deeply inside her body that it made her heart trip erratically. He reached her womb and beyond, she had no doubt.

He was so thick. So long. She'd never expected just how massive he would be.

Mia felt the first twinges of her orgasm with something like surprise. She'd never come without using a vibrator or her own fingers before. She hadn't believed it would be possible to come just from Ryan's thrusting dick inside of her, but it was.

Her body tensed then began to shake. Her hands fell to the bed and fisted there. She cried out and Ryan drank in the sound with his mouth over hers. He thrust harder into her, bringing her legs up higher around his waist so that he slid impossibly deeper into her body.

Ecstasy unimaginable flooded through her. Her head and fingers and toes felt as though light shone through from them. She was on fire.

She *was* on fire!

Mia gasped and tamped down on the flames that had already begun to lick up her arms. The flames disappeared, but not before she'd singed holes into the comforter beneath them.

Ryan seemed not to notice or care, increasing the pace of his thrusts. His hips pistoned between her legs like a jackhammer. His fingers found a nipple and her clit and he rubbed both at the same time. Mia arched up sharply and came again, the bright starlight of completion blinding her to all else.

She milked his cock with her muscles, and with a grunt Ryan jettisoned his own release deep within her. The hot, creamy splash of his cum filled her to overflowing, making both their bodies wet with his essence. Ryan's head lay on the pillow beside hers, his lungs bellowing for air.

"Was I too rough?" he asked softly at her ear.

Mia once more wound her arms tightly around him and his cock slid deeper into her wetness. "No, you weren't too rough at all," she assured him.

He pulled back and looked down at her, his blue eyes bright and intent. He stroked his thumb across her lips and she darted her tongue out to taste him. He tasted like her.

"I've wanted to do that forever," he admitted.

"Me too." She smiled.

"I love you," he whispered, and her smile disappeared.

"No you don't. Don't say that," she said, pulling away from him, gasping when his cock popped out of her and gaining her feet by the bed.

"I do love you," he insisted, doing nothing to stop her as she began getting dressed in his damp, discarded clothing.

"Don't say that," she yelled, then immediately sobered. "I don't need you to love me in order to fuck me."

Ryan gritted his teeth. "That's not what I meant—"

"I know what you meant. Let it rest, all right? You don't love me. You're just…infatuated, that's all. It's hormones."

"This isn't hormones and you know it," he growled.

Mia left the room without saying anything further and Ryan teleported himself directly into her path as she made her way toward the door. "Don't leave like this," he warned.

"Don't pull this disappearing, reappearing shit with me, Ryan." She held up her hand and let a lick of violet flame sprout from her fingertips. "Or did you forget that we're unevenly matched here?"

"You wouldn't hurt me," he scoffed confidently, shoving her hand aside, paying no attention to the flame that spurted and went out. "Not like that."

Mia looked away from his all too knowing eyes.

"Why don't you want to hear that I'm in love with you?"

Mia put her hands up to her ears in a childish gesture even she knew would be ineffective. "You're not in love with me," she insisted.

Ryan's gaze burned hers. "I'll prove it to you."

Mia shook her head. "No. I don't want you to prove it to me. I don't want you to love me. If you say it one more time I'll never sleep with you again."

"You've never slept with me to begin with."

"You're right. I *fucked* you. There, are those bald enough words for you?" she demanded stubbornly, reaching around him for the door handle.

"You know that's not what I want to hear. Why can't you just accept the fact that I do care for you?"

"Oh I've no doubt that you care for me. But you don't love me."

Ryan's teeth gritted so hard she heard them. "Why are you being like this?"

"Because I have to be," she said softly and moved around him determinedly. "I'll see you later, Ryan." She opened the door and stepped through it. Ryan followed her, uncaring of his nudity.

"Don't be like this, Mia," he called out.

She broke into a run and made it to her apartment in record time, shutting the door as if that might keep him out. She leaned back against it and a broken, hopeless sob escaped her.

What had she just done?

Chapter Four

೫

Mia refused to see Ryan for two days. He came by every half hour it seemed to bang on her door and demand that she let him come in. He could have simply teleported himself into her room, but he didn't seem inclined to, no matter how desperately he seemed to want to see her. He tirelessly visited her, never once giving up.

She would have gone home but something held her back. She didn't know what, but it was stronger than her will to leave Sterling and Ryan behind.

She just couldn't run from him. Not like this. She could hardly live with herself as it was, and she didn't think she could handle adding abandonment to her list of transgressions.

Why had she turned away from his declaration of love? She had some idea. It shamed her that she'd loved him since childhood and now, when afforded the opportunity, she had backed away from the face of that truth. But Mia just couldn't be close to anybody, no matter how desperately she might want to be.

She was a dangerous person to be around. There was always the risk that she might have another accident and kill whoever might be with her at the time. She just couldn't risk it.

But oh how she wanted to.

She couldn't gamble with Ryan's life like that. No matter how much she wanted him.

She'd almost had an attack in bed with him. It had taken a great act of will to dampen the flames that had licked up her arms toward Ryan. She couldn't—*wouldn't*—begin to imagine what would happen if she had an accident in her sleep while lying beside him.

It had been years since the last time she'd had an attack during sleep. But she knew how little that meant in the grand scheme of things. She'd thought her accidents were over. How wrong she'd been. And now she knew she had to turn away from the only man she'd ever loved, the only man she'd ever made love with, in order to keep him safe.

Mia wouldn't be able to live with herself if she hurt Ryan in any way. It would simply be too much for her to bear.

On her second day of silent seclusion there came a knock at her door, and it wasn't Ryan.

Mia opened the door to find Steele standing on the other side, waiting patiently. Steele was always patient. Normally it would have been soothing for her to see him, but today she merely wanted to get rid of him. She didn't want a lecture, and Steele was very good at giving them.

"We're having a meeting," he told her.

Mia frowned. "About what?"

"Siren. They're up to something. Something big. We'd all be grateful if you'd come and offer some input."

"Who's meeting with you?"

"Ryan, John Spada, his wife Enya and my wife Marla."

Feeling guilty, Mia winced. "I'm sorry. I haven't met your wife yet. She must think I'm the rudest person on earth."

"She understands. I've told her that we grew up together, and I explained about your talents. Marla has her own unique abilities. She understands that you need a little time for yourself."

Mia breathed a heavy sigh. "I guess I could come. I'm not doing anything else."

Steele smiled. "Don't be worried. Ryan won't cause a scene in front of everyone."

She grimaced. "Do you know everything that goes on here, Steele?"

He chuckled. "I make it a point to. It saves a lot of explanations, don't you think?"

Mia ignored him. "Give me five minutes to get ready, okay?"

Steele nodded and let her close the door. She heard him whistling as she went about getting properly dressed for a Sterling meeting.

* * * * *

Ryan saw Mia walk into the room and felt something like a swift blow in his midsection. He'd been trying for two days to see her, but she hadn't let him. Now she walked in with Steele, and if Ryan didn't know better he would have been jealous. The only thing keeping him from blowing up at his friend was that he knew Steele was very happily married and not in the market for a girlfriend.

Steele introduced her to his wife first thing as they all gathered around Ryan's desk. Mia smiled, looking lovelier to him than ever before, and shook Marla's hand. Next she was introduced to Johnny Vicious—or John Spada, as he was also called—and his wife Enya. This gave Ryan enough time to school his features into a blank mask. He didn't want anyone to know what was going on between him and Mia.

But it seemed that everyone already did—Sterling wasn't so big, after all. News traveled fast. Especially when it was about Ryan. And Ryan could see by the glances cast his way that his friends had already heard about their standoff and what had ultimately caused it.

Mia refused to look at him. She sat down in a chair offered to her by Vicious and waited for the meeting to begin.

Ryan cleared his throat. "Well, we'll get right down to it then. We've received information that Siren is going to market their cerebral enhancing chips to the public."

Mia started and finally looked at him. "What chips?"

Ryan caught her gaze with his and held it.

Steele, sensing a storm brewing in the wind, took over. "Siren has created microchips that can be attached to the scalp. The chip sends electron beacons through the skull to the brain. They're supposed to improve motor skills and brain power. And I suppose in some ways they do. But what the chips also do is cause massive brain damage, even hemorrhaging in some cases."

"My God," Mia breathed. "How are they getting government approval to bring this thing to market?"

"We don't know. Maybe they haven't. But what we *do* know is that the public must absolutely be kept away from these chips. They're a disaster waiting to happen in more ways than one," Ryan offered.

"How do you expect to keep them from releasing the chips?" Marla asked.

Johnny Vicious, an extremely tall man in a black trench coat, spoke up. "We know where they're working on the chips. We can strike at their compound and destroy the technology."

Steele ran a hand over his shaved head. "How do you propose we do such a thing?"

"We wait until tonight. Have Marla use her gift to shut off the power at the compound. Then the rest of us can slip in with flame throwers and torch the place."

Mia, who knew about the vigilante work at Sterling, wasn't surprised by this suggestion. "I could help with that."

Ryan shook his head. "You're not going." His gaze rested on the other women present and it became clear he included them in his statement.

Mia surged up from her seat. "You can't stop me from going."

"Me either," Enya stepped beside her.

Marla joined them. "We're all going."

Vicious chuckled.

Steele scowled.

Ryan gritted his teeth and looked into Mia's eyes. "Fine. You can all go. And hey, why not invite everyone at Sterling? Let's just make a party out of it while we're at it."

"Shut up, Ryan," Vicious grinned devilishly. "Give in gracefully for once."

Ryan ran a hand through his already disheveled blond hair. "I don't think this is a good idea."

"Nor do I," Steele agreed.

"Let's take a vote on it," Enya suggested.

Ryan sighed. "We won't need a vote. Oh boy. All right. You win. We'll strike at them tonight, while there are fewer people about. But," he warned, "you'll follow my orders once we're in. I don't want to allow for any accidents to happen, is that clear?"

Mia knew he wasn't referring to her, but it still stung to hear those words. She could control her gifts to a point—beyond that it was all a luck of the draw. She couldn't guarantee that she'd be successful in this venture. But she could at least try. And she would.

"We'll need to destroy their entire lab to get rid of all the information they've researched about these chips. And that's no guarantee that they won't try this again in the future, once their scientists have engineered new chips," Steele said.

"I can do that," Mia said softly.

"Are you sure?" Steele searched her face for an answer.

"I'm sure," she replied firmly. "But after that...I can't really promise anything."

Steele nodded. He was more than familiar with how volatile and unpredictable her powers could be. "We'll try and stay out of your way."

"Well, this was an easy meeting," Vicious quipped with a wink in his wife's direction. "When do we get started?"

"We'll meet in the parking lot at eleven and make our move then. I expect to be in and out of there by midnight," Ryan said decisively.

"That's cutting it a little close, don't you think?" Steele frowned.

"We have to cut it close. I don't want any of us to dawdle. We can't be found before the chips are destroyed."

"He's right," Mia pointed out. "And the fewer who know it was us that struck at them, the better."

"Until tonight then." Johnny gave a jaunty wave and grabbed his wife's hand. He practically dragged her from the room.

Steele wasn't too far behind. He tucked his wife beneath his arm and walked through the door. "Tonight at eleven then," he nodded at Mia and Ryan. Then they were gone, closing the door softly behind them.

Mia stood frozen, wanting to stay but also wanting to leave.

Ryan watched her for a long moment. "Don't you dare leave," he growled at last.

"I need to go rest up if I'm going to be of any use to you tonight," she said weakly.

His eyes filled with an inner fire. "How about being of use to me now?"

"What do you mean?" She backed cautiously away from the desk.

His face grew hard. Impassive. "Take your clothes off," he commanded. "*Now.*"

Chapter Five

ഏ

Mia backed toward the door, but there was no use in running. Ryan teleported to stand in her way, and barred what would have been her hasty retreat out of there and away from the smoldering passion evident in his eyes. Mia turned around and there he was before her again.

"Stop it right this instant, Ryan."

"If you search inside yourself you'll realize that you don't want me to stop. *Ever*. Now...your clothes."

Ryan grabbed the hem of her sweater and pulled it over her head before she could protest, leaving her lacy bra exposed to his hungry gaze. Mia grabbed at the sweater and tried to put it back on, so Ryan snatched it back from her and threw it across the room. "Take the rest of your clothes off now or I'll do it for you," he said roughly.

"Quit acting like a brute," she growled.

Ryan's eyes darkened ominously. "I'm not acting at all. I *am* a brute. You should always remember that."

Mia felt liquid heat pool between her legs. "I'm not having sex with you in this office. Someone's bound to come in—"

"No one will come in. And if they did...would you really mind that much, having an audience?"

Mia shivered. She put her hands behind her back and unhooked her bra. She watched as Ryan licked his lips, eying her every movement. She held the bra aloft between two fingers and let it drop to the floor. Ryan's eyes followed its descent but swiftly turned back to gaze ravenously at her nude breasts.

"You have the prettiest nipples I've ever seen," he said. "And the sweetest. I could suck on them all day."

He came forward and put his hands beneath the hem of the skirt she wore. He lifted it up to reveal her prim, white cotton panties. "Your pussy is so juicy, so soft. So tight." He hooked his fingers inside the elastic of her panties and stroked her erotically. Teasingly.

The deep blue of his eyes had turned almost black. He bent his head and laid his forehead against hers. "I had blood on my cock when you left me the last time," he whispered. He lightly traced his lips across her brow. "Were you a virgin, Mia mine?"

Mia stiffened. "What kind of question is that?" she evaded.

One corner of Ryan's mouth lifted in a lopsided grin. "You know what kind of question it is. The truth now. Were you a virgin?"

"So what if I was," Mia said proudly. "I'm not anymore."

Ryan's eyes closed as if he was savoring her words. When he opened them a self-satisfied spark had entered his gaze. "Am I the only one who's ever touched your sweet breasts before? Am I the first person to touch your wet, hot pussy?"

Mia snorted. "Don't be so smug. So you're the first, what does it matter?" She felt her wicked juices boiling. "Besides, you won't be the last," she lied.

Ryan's eyes grew stormy, furious even. He pushed her roughly back against the wall and tore her panties from her with a sharp, tearing sound. He shoved her skirt up around her waist and pressed himself between her legs. He rubbed against her, pressing his arousal hard into her belly and cunt.

"Don't say things like that, Mia. Else I might believe them," he whispered, the softness of his words belying the ruthless, bruising grip he had on her upper arms.

His hand moved up to fist in her hair. He wrapped the long locks around his wrist and hand, holding her head still as he gazed down at her. "You're mine now, Mia. There's no going back."

Mia felt her heart skip a beat. "Who said I wanted to go back?" She watched his face for some emotion other than frustrated anger. "I like not being a virgin."

"You know what I meant. You're mine. No one else's. We'll get married as soon as possible."

"The hell you say!" she exploded, pushing back against him though he was as immovable as a mountain and he barely seemed to notice her struggles. "No way will I marry you."

"Why not?" he asked. "You like fucking me. I'm certain of that much." He leaned in closer to her ear. One of his fingers wandered into the slit of her pussy and sought out her clit. "You're wet and sticky for me already. You can't deny your attraction to me."

Mia undulated against his hand, helpless in a sea of pleasure that threatened to drown her. "I do like fucking you. And you like it too. So why don't you just shut up and dick me down?"

Ryan's eyes flashed. "That will be my pleasure," he growled. His hands went to the fastening of his jeans and he brought out the heavy, turgid length of his cock. "Look at it. It's weeping with need for you," he whispered.

It was true. A solitary tear had formed at the head of his penis and was dripping down the crown and onto the length of his shaft.

"Are you ready to learn how to suck me off?" he asked oh so softly.

Shaking with desire, she nodded, beyond words. Ryan put his hands back on her shoulders and pushed her down. She sank to her knees before him. His long, thick cock bobbed like a wand toward her mouth. He put his hands in her hair and gently but demandingly pulled her face closer to it.

"Open your mouth. Wide," he commanded, looking down at her from his great height.

Mia pressed a tiny kiss to the head of his cock and sipped at the tear that fell from it. He tasted wild, like summer rain and sweet honeysuckle nectar. She'd never expected him to taste so good.

His fingers pressed into the corners of her mouth and she opened it wide.

"Be careful of your teeth," he cautioned before slipping the mushroomed head past her lips and into her mouth. Mia opened wider and he slipped deeper into her mouth, touching the back of her throat.

She swirled her tongue around him, catching his full masculine flavor. She sucked him, gently at first, then harder. Ryan groaned and pushed her hair back away from her face to better see what she was doing. His cock had nearly disappeared inside her greedy mouth, and he moaned at the sight of her rooting there against him.

Mia cupped his testicles in her palm, gently massaging them. She learned the technique fast, pumping his cock with her hand and mouth while playing with his sac. Ryan shuddered against her.

"No, stop," he said, pushing her away.

But Mia would not be stopped. She latched onto his dick, slurping it deep into the back of her throat. Ryan shouted, pumped his hips fast three times against her face and shot his sweet load down her throat. He tasted magical. She drank every drop he had to give and sucked him clean for more.

Ryan lifted her up in his arms. She wrapped her legs around his waist. His cock, so amazingly thick, slid into her sharply. Mia caught her breath at the heavy, burning feel of him filling her. Her body, already damp with need, grew impossibly wetter, until their bodies were slippery with her juices.

The sounds their bodies made as he began thrusting inside of her swamped both their ears. Mia moaned and wrapped her arms and legs tighter around him. Ryan lifted her higher then slammed her down upon him. Mia keened wildly and hung on for dear life.

His hips jackhammered in and out of her body. He lifted her high and found her nipple with his mouth. He used his teeth against her, biting her gently, leaving his marks behind. Mia shuddered and rode him like a stallion, bouncing easily up and down his length, impaling herself over and over again.

Her clit brushed against the fur of his sex and soon it was tingling and swelling. With every thrust he made, her clit sang with ecstasy. Ryan began to thrust even harder into her. Mia felt her pussy clench — once, twice — and then she found the pinnacle of passion.

She screamed, bumping and grinding her pussy against him. He held her in his strong arms, never letting go, allowing her to find her pleasure.

Ryan groaned long and loud and came inside of her. His cum burned her and filled her full to overflowing. Mia cried out again and fell limply against him. Her body, covered in perspiration, shivered in the sudden coolness of the air. Ryan pumped himself into her over and over, emptying himself deep. Then he collapsed, sinking to his knees, still holding her and gasping for breath.

"You will marry me, Mia," he said at length.

Mia pulled out of his arms and gathered her scattered clothing, dressing silently.

"You can't ignore me forever," he pointed out. "And I'm not going to change my mind."

"Stop saying such things, Ryan. You can't mean them. We're too different, you and I."

"Opposites attract, or hadn't you heard?"

"We're not even opposites. You've got your life wrapped up here in Sterling, as it should be. I don't want any part of that."

"You used to love it here." He adjusted himself and fastened his pants, watching her.

Mia shrugged. "I did love it here. But after nearly hurting Steele I realized how dangerous it was for me to stay here among so many people that could get hurt or even killed if I lost control. You and I can never be together here."

"You don't know that."

Mia nodded. "Yes I do."

"I love you." He said it almost wearily.

"No you don't." She gritted her teeth.

"Stop being so stubborn." He ran a frustrated hand through his hair. "Admit that you have feelings for me too."

Mia squeezed her eyes shut tightly and tried to slow the swift galloping of her heart. "No, Ryan."

"There's so much between us—"

"No there isn't. We've just had sex a couple of times, that's all."

Ryan growled. "It wasn't just sex and you know it."

She did know it. And it made it all the harder to stand firm with him now. But she had to. For his own safety as well as hers. "Let it go, Ryan."

"I'll let it go for now, but you'll have to admit it to me sooner or later, and when you do I'll find the nearest priest and marry you right on the spot."

Mia laughed and shook her head. "You always were a persistent one."

"Funny how some things never change."

He moved to let her pass and she made it to the door, not daring to look back. She paused before closing it behind her. "I'm sorry, Ryan. I just can't give you what you're looking for."

She closed the door and felt something inside her soul close off as well. Not that her feelings mattered. All that mattered was that Ryan and the others at Sterling remain safe. After their mission tonight, she was going to ensure that they stayed that way.

It was time for her to go home.

Chapter Six

ഔ

That night the six of them gathered in the Sterling parking lot and loaded up into Steele's Expedition. They didn't bring many weapons. Gifted people like themselves rarely had a need for them. Johnny Vicious had two massive hand cannons and Ryan had a Beretta. That was about it. And that should have been all that was necessary. They weren't going to kill anybody, just destroy a little property.

Mia sat in the far backseat with Marla. Vicious and Enya sat in the next seat and Ryan and Steele had the front.

"I hear you're a pyrokenetic," Marla said.

"I am," Mia replied softly.

"That's pretty amazing."

"What gifts do you have?" Mia asked, curious.

"I interfere with electromagnetic waves. I can pretty much fry any piece of electrical equipment you could come up with. I had a hard time controlling it at first, bursting light bulbs in my home, turning the TV on and off with my mind...you know, things like that. But the scientists at Sterling made this bracelet for me, which keeps me grounded. Or something to that effect. Whatever, it helps me control my powers."

"No one's ever found anything to help me control my quirks."

Marla put her arm around Mia's shoulders gently. "That must be tough."

"It can be," Mia admitted.

"At least you've got like-minded people here at Sterling to relate to."

Ryan must have heard Marla's words because he turned around and locked his gaze with Mia's. Something dark and dangerous swam in the depths of his amazing blue eyes. Mia looked away and stared out the window, watching the dark road as they drove toward Siren's headquarters in downtown Akron. When she looked back Ryan was facing forward once more.

It was only a twenty-five-minute drive to Siren's compound. They all spent the trip in relative silence, steeling themselves for what they must do. The trip was over too fast for Mia, who knew she had perhaps the biggest part to play in their mission.

The compound's parking lot was gated and Steele parked his vehicle just outside it. Everyone filed out of the enormous SUV and took stock of their situation.

"Do we know where we're headed?" Mia asked.

"I've studied the entire layout of this place," Ryan said. "I'm certain we'll find the right lab where the chips are being stored and catalogued. All evidence of the technology should be within the lab. If we're lucky."

Mia nodded. She watched as Vicious' hands went behind his back and toyed with the two guns there. She knew that Vicious was known for his incredible, preternatural speed. She'd seen evidence of it herself in the past twenty-four hours. Sometimes when he moved he seemed to blur and then he'd appear somewhere else. It was unnerving. She wondered if he was equally as fast with his guns.

They were all dressed in black, right down to the crocheted cap Mia had put over her too bright blonde hair. They approached the fence and Ryan produced a pair of wire cutters. He made short work of the fence, cutting a hole big enough that even Steele could fit through and tossed the cutters back into the SUV.

"I'll check for guards," Johnny whispered and took off, moving so fast none of them saw him as he darted deeper onto the compound's grounds. Several minutes passed in tense silence before he returned. "We're lucky. There were only two guards. I took care of them. They'll wake up with headaches but they'll be fine."

"Are we ready?" Ryan asked them.

They all agreed that they were. "It's now or never," Steele said.

They crept through the fence and made their way across the lot to the expansive building that was the Siren compound. There were few lights on within it, and it seemed to be deserted. It was a lucky break for them. They came upon a door. Ryan teleported into the building, reappearing behind the door and unlocking it for his comrades, letting them inside.

They were silent as the grave as they made their way deeper into the compound. They passed office after office, down one winding hallway and the next. Ryan seemed confident that he was leading them the right way. He never faltered or paused to get his bearings. Mia caught herself staring at his delectable rear as they walked, and looked away guiltily.

Now was not the time to get her hormones in an uproar.

The building was vast, nearly as big as Sterling, and by the time they'd reached the heart of it Mia was completely lost as to how to get back. She supposed it didn't matter. Ryan was the expert on the floor plans—he'd get them out without a problem. Still, it made Mia uneasy.

"I think this is the primary lab," Ryan said as they neared an enormous room with glass walls. Beyond it lay dozens of computers and various pieces of laboratory equipment. It was devoid of people. Mia gave a sigh of relief.

Ryan did his disappearing trick again and unlocked the doors. Mia stepped into the room first, looking around curiously. Since she'd first been brought to Sterling as a child, she'd known about Siren. They'd seemed so dark and mysterious to her in those years. Sterling's nemesis in all things,

Siren had often had spies planted within Sterling. They'd vandalized Sterling more than once.

Now it was time to turn the tables on them.

Ryan sat before a computer and began inputting data. Mia looked around, assuring herself that what she was about to do was totally necessary. She found a large filing cabinet in one corner and opened one of its many drawers. There were hundreds of names on hundreds of folders, but she didn't recognize any of them.

She pulled one folder out at random and looked within. The file contained detailed medical descriptions and patient information. She looked at one particular piece of paper and was surprised to see that "cerebral" chips were mentioned more than once.

"Hey guys, listen to this," she called out softly. "'Patient experienced epileptic seizure and toxic shock. Cerebral chip has been rejected and removed. No further study necessary.' So does that mean not everyone can wear the chips?"

"No, not all," Steele replied. "But most. The first crop of chips actually caused trauma and even death in patients, which might be the case here. The newest chips are better suited for human wear but are still far too dangerous both to the patient and to the public around them."

Mia put the folder back and closed the drawer.

"Ryan, are you getting anywhere?" Marla asked.

"Just a minute. These files are encrypted. It's going to take a bit of troubleshooting."

Mia moved to a cabinet and opened the heavy wooden doors. Inside was tray after tray of microchips. "Hey, is this what we're looking for?"

Steele came up behind her. "Yeah, these are what we're after." He reached beyond her shoulder and took a chip between two fingers. He studied it closely for a minute then crumbled it in his fist. "I hope this is all they've produced so far."

"How can we be sure?" Mia asked.

Steele sighed heavily. "We can't. We can only pray that they haven't already begun mass production for the open market."

"I'm in," Ryan said, breaking into their conversation. "Here's everything, every little test done using the chips, every failure, every success. They've had no shortage of test subjects, or so it seems here. Hopefully they were willing subjects."

"I wouldn't count on it with Siren," Marla drawled.

"Let me just print some of this stuff out and then we can get down to the real business here." Ryan began transferring files to be printed.

Mia saw a movement out of the corner of her eye. "Hide," she hissed and immediately ducked as someone walked by in the darkness.

Everyone went to the floor at Mia's warning. But it was no use. The door to the lab opened and on came the lights.

Chapter Seven

છ

"Hey, what's going on here?" A lab technician in a white coat stepped into the room.

Mia didn't need to be told what to do. She turned toward the cabinet which housed the chips and flung her hands out. Violet flames jettisoned from her fingertips, engulfing the wood in a blazing hot fire.

Another technician entered the room behind the first. He yelled at Mia to stop and rushed her. Ryan stepped into his path and punched him squarely on the jaw, knocking him unconscious. The first technician dove toward one of the desks and pressed a button.

Loud sirens screamed into the night.

"Shit," Mia said, and turned to lay a path of fire from one end of the lab to the other. "Get them out of here," she told Steele, referring to both her colleagues and the two lab technicians. "I've got this."

The technician who'd hit the alarm scampered back as Steele advanced upon him. "Get out," he said ominously, commandingly. The lab technician took one look at Mia, her arms engulfed in violet flame, and turned to run from the room.

The sounds of approaching people reached Mia's ears. "Get out of here," she yelled.

Ryan grabbed his printouts and came to her side. "Come on," he urged, grabbing her upper arm, careful of the flames that licked up her forearms.

"You said all evidence of these chips needs to be destroyed. Go. Get the others out of here. I won't be far behind you."

"I'm not leaving without you," Ryan protested, tugging on her harder.

Mia felt the fire within her burn hot. She felt her hair stand on end beneath her cap and she tore it from her head. Seconds later a halo of fire swept around her head. "Go!" she screamed at Ryan, breaking free. "Go now before someone gets hurt."

Ryan hesitated then turned to the others. "Let's get out of here."

Mia laid a carpet of fire along the room. The flames licked at her friends' feet as they fled but did not penetrate beyond the room. Mia gave a silent prayer of thanks that she hadn't totally lost control yet.

A gunshot startled her and she watched as two guards gave chase to her friends. She yelled for them to stop, but flames licked up and filled her mouth, cutting off her words. She saw Ryan disappear around a corner and tried to dispel the flames still shooting in bursts from her fingertips.

Nothing happened.

Mia felt her entire body engulf in heat. She was losing it. She'd never pushed herself so hard before. Never had to test her skills in a combat situation. She wasn't going to be able to hold it back much longer.

She made it to the center of the room before the glass walls exploded outward. Mia would have screamed if she could. Flames licked their way up the hallway, eating up the walls like slithering violet serpents. Mia fled from the room, but the flames followed her. She couldn't control them anymore.

Her body felt as if it were full to bursting. She let it go, knowing it would only hurt if she fought it. She hoped her friends were outside because it wasn't just the lab that was going to go up in flames. A flood of fire spilled out of her, filling the hallway. She tried to run from it but there was no escape.

The floor rumbled beneath her feet.

An earsplitting roar filled her ears.

The building exploded.

Shards of glass and wood joined the flames shooting high into the air before raining back down about her. She ran through the wreckage, sobbing for breath that didn't taste like fire. Fire was everywhere now, all around. Mia turned this way and that, searching for a way out. The flames consuming her stuttered then went out.

She saw a shaft of moonlight through a particularly thick pile of wreckage. Mia ran to it and began tossing pieces of wood and brick behind her. She dug her way through, exiting head first into the night air beyond. She ran down the side of the burning building, looking for a way to escape the grounds, looking for her friends.

She didn't see the parking lot—she was too far into the compound. But she saw a road several hundred yards out. She ran full tilt, arms and legs pumping. She was running from more than just the fire and the wreckage of the building.

She was running away from herself.

* * * * *

"I have to go back and get her," Ryan yelled, struggling in Steele's grip.

"She'll be fine. Mia can take care of herself. We have to get out of here now." Steele forcibly dragged Ryan into the Expedition.

"At least we don't have to worry about surveillance tapes now," Vicious said, looking back at the still-blazing wreckage.

"Get in," Steele commanded, cranking the engine and revving it high. Vicious hopped into the SUV and before he'd even closed the door, tires squealed and they were off.

They made it to the main road, Steele driving the vehicle over curbs and grass to reach it. They hadn't traveled more than a couple hundred yards when they saw Mia running down the expressway.

Steele slammed on the brakes and parked in the emergency lane. Ryan was out of the vehicle before it had even stopped. He ran to Mia, who didn't stop as she passed him at a full sprint. He ran to catch up with her. "Mia," he called out, "stop! It's me."

But Mia paid him no heed—she simply kept running as if she never meant to stop. Ryan ran at her side, trying to catch her in his arms. He grabbed her, swinging her around to face him.

Mia screamed and batted him away, turning and running once more.

"Mia, it's all right," he called out, but to no avail. He ran once more to catch up with her. Steele's SUV crept behind them at a crawl.

"Fuck it," he said, and teleported himself directly into her path. "Stop, Mia," he said, grabbing her in an iron grip.

Mia sobbed and collapsed against him. He lifted her up into his arms and walked back to the SUV. He sat her in the middle seat and crawled in with her. "It's going to be all right honey. I promise," he cajoled soothingly.

"No it's not," she cried. "Did you see what just happened? What I just did? I'm a monster!"

"You're not a monster," both Steele and Ryan said in unison.

"Look, honey, you're not a monster. Everything's going to be fine, you'll see."

"I want to die," she sobbed.

Ryan's hands bit into her upper arms. "No. Don't you dare say such a thing! I won't stand for it, do you hear me?" He shook her lightly.

Mia's tear-swamped eyes rose to meet his. "I'm never going to be normal, am I?"

"Mia, Mia," he crooned, pulling her into the protection of his embrace. "You're as normal as any of us in this vehicle now. Don't do this to yourself. It's killing me to see you so unhappy."

"I just wanted to be of some help," she whispered brokenly, putting her head in her hands.

"You were," Vicious said from the seat behind them. "We won't have to worry about Siren for a long time now."

Ryan glared at him and Vicious subsided, looking out the window as if he hadn't a care in the world.

"Shh, baby, don't cry," Ryan said, using his sleeve to wipe away her tears. "It's all right."

"All I ever wanted was to be normal," she said softly.

"I know," Ryan held her tighter. "But it's just not in the cards. For either of us."

Mia gathered herself and pulled away from him. "Did anyone get hurt?"

"I don't think so. There were only a few people there and they all seemed to be filing out of the building as fast as we were."

Mia nodded. "Thank God."

"Do you think Siren will strike back?" Marla asked from the front passenger seat.

"Who knows?" Ryan said. "They may not even realize for a time that we were involved. We can at least hope for that. We all knew going into this that there was the possibility of retribution. Violence is all Siren is good at anyway, I think."

Mia fell into a deep silence, eyes vacant and unblinking. Ryan gathered her closer and held her, knowing it was what she needed most.

The rest of the drive was spent in a heavy silence that consumed them all.

Chapter Eight

ഔ

Ryan was at her door again. It was a wonder to her that he hadn't simply teleported himself inside, but she supposed he was trying to be respectful of her privacy.

It had been three days since the disaster at Siren and she still couldn't bring herself to face the others. She would have long ago left for home if there wasn't the chance of seeing someone on her way out. As it was, she was trapped in her apartment, brooding and suffering from dark thoughts.

She'd almost killed them all.

Mia couldn't live with herself knowing this. She prayed that everyone had escaped from the fire at Siren. There hadn't been any reports of deaths in the newspaper article covering the fire. But the entire Siren compound was in ashes. The fire had burned long into the night, resistant to the water and fire extinguishers the firemen had used in their attempt to put it out. They'd had to let the blaze run its course. And it had, eating away all evidence of the once vast building.

No attempts yet had been made on Siren's part to seek revenge against Sterling. There wasn't even evidence that suggested they knew Sterling was behind the strike. But that didn't mean they wouldn't come calling, one day down the road. And it wouldn't be pretty.

"Mia, I know you're listening to me. Open this door right now," Ryan called, breaking into her reverie.

Mia leaned back against the couch and waited for him to leave.

He didn't.

"I'm coming in there," he warned, and a second later there he stood before her. "Why are you in here brooding?" he demanded, coming down on one knee beside her.

"I'm not brooding," she lied.

"You're a terrible liar," he pointed out, touching his finger to the dimple in her chin.

"I don't know what to do anymore, Ryan," she admitted. "I can't go on like this."

He didn't pretend to misunderstand her. "Then let our scientists continue to work with you. Eventually they'll find a way to help you control your powers."

Mia shook her head. "No more tests, they don't do any good."

"We helped Marla. We can help you. Just give us a chance. Give *me* a chance."

"I could've killed those people," she sobbed. "I could've killed you."

"But you didn't."

"Not this time. But what about the next time? And the next? Can you assure me that I won't accidentally kill anyone?"

"Mia, it won't do you any good to keep yourself secluded in here like a hermit. It won't do you any good to worry about what might or might not happen in the future. Hell, I might die of a brain aneurism at any moment, but I'm not worried about it. Neither should you be. Just live. Live and be happy with the time you're given."

"I can't be like that," she whispered brokenly.

"Yes you can."

Mia sniffed and wiped away her tears. "What about the others? Are they afraid of me now?"

"No one is afraid of you. You're not a monster," he patiently pointed out. "You're just different. There's nothing wrong with that."

"That's what your dad always used to tell me."

"Truer words were never spoken." He tucked an errant strand of hair behind her ear. "Now, are you going to let this rule your life? Or are you going to come out with me and have a fabulous dinner at my place?"

Mia smiled. "Well, since you put it like that…"

"I love you, Mia."

She shied away from him. "Don't say that."

"But it's true."

Mia looked at him. Her heart felt broken in two. She couldn't look him in the eye and lie anymore, though she desperately wanted to. She was tired of lying. Tired of hiding. But she didn't know what else to do—she was so used to it at this point.

His gaze locked with hers. "I love you. I do. And I promise I'll do anything for you, anything to help you get over and through this. I can't stand to see you so torn up."

"Ryan, I can't love you," she whispered.

"Yes you can. You do. I can see it in your eyes, even if you're too afraid to say the words."

"We could never be. I can't go through life wondering when my next accident will happen and whether or not you'll be hurt by it."

"Life is about taking chances," he pointed out.

"I know." She looked down at her hands. Ryan reached up and took them in his.

"Look at me."

She did.

"No matter what happens, I'll always love you. I *have* always loved you. Nothing can change that."

Mia's lip trembled. "It's too dangerous."

Ryan pressed his lips to their clasped hands. "No it's not. Nothing is too dangerous when love is involved."

Mia felt torn. She loved him. She'd loved him for years. But she knew she couldn't tell him—he'd never let her forget it. She didn't want that, she wanted to know that he was safe, even if that meant she had to be apart from him.

"Make love to me," she whispered.

Ryan took a deep breath. "Is that what you want?"

"Yes." She held his hands tight.

Ryan leaned in and kissed her, his tongue stroking her bottom lip. He put his hands beneath her T-shirt and found her bare breasts with his palms. He leaned her back onto the couch and pushed her shirt up high.

He dipped down for a taste of her nipple. He slurped one into his mouth, suckling it before visiting the same upon the other. He shoved his hand into the waistband of her pants and cupped her cunt with his warm palm.

He tore his mouth away from her and tore at his clothes. She helped him as best she could, pushing his sweater up so that she could tease and taste his small brown nipples. In seconds he was nude and working on making her much the same.

He spread her legs wide and pressed his lips to her aching pussy. His lips found her clit and suckled on it as he had suckled her nipples. He shoved two fingers into her pleasure hole and slipped a third into her anus. Mia cried out and tried to pull away, but he wouldn't let her, holding her fast.

He opened his mouth over her. He thrust his fingers in and out of her body until she was dripping with need. He lifted her hips and licked her anus, wetting it, then inserted two fingers into her.

Mia cried out as an orgasm shook her, making her pussy clench and milk his probing tongue as it stabbed into the heat of her.

"Oh Ryan, yes!" she cried.

"Tell me you love me," he demanded, his lips and words vibrating against her pussy.

Mia bucked wildly beneath him. "No," she choked out.

"Yes," he said, licking her from clit to anus. "Say it."

"Please fuck me, Ryan!"

"I'll fuck you. I'll fuck you until you don't know anything but my touch anymore."

He crawled up her body, tugging her legs around his hips. She locked her ankles behind his waist and screamed as he entered her in one long push of his hips.

He pumped himself into her, stretching and filling her until she was mindless to anything else. Her head thrashed back and forth on the cushions and she bucked and undulated in tune to his body's thrusts into hers.

Ryan pulled away with a savage curse. He turned her over and entered her from behind. Mia saw stars as he reached deeper inside of her than he ever had before. He rode her, balls slapping against her pussy and legs. She moved with him, seeking each new impalement as if it would be her last.

"Oh God, Ryan, you feel so good," she gasped.

"I love how tight and hot you are," he said, biting her shoulder. "How wet and silky you feel."

Her body shivered.

He slammed into her harder and harder. She cried out as she experienced the most explosive orgasm of her life. Ryan followed her seconds later, groaning and gasping as he pumped his cum deep into her welcoming body.

Ryan rose and lifted her up off the couch. He let her wrap her legs around him and entered her standing up. He walked them to her bedroom and laid them both down on the bed. He moved in her softly, soothingly, semi-hard and gentle within her still quivering body.

They lay there, damp bodies joined, and just before sleep consumed him he heard her soft, hesitant whisper.

"I love you, Ryan. I really, really do."

He fell asleep with a smile on his face.

When Ryan awoke she had gone. Gone from Sterling. Gone from him. He swore a blue streak and rose to get dressed for battle.

Chapter Nine

ഇ

Ryan knocked on Mia's door demandingly. "Open up or I'm opening it for you."

Mia opened the door. She must have been standing right behind it when he approached.

"What's this?" She frowned, squinting up in the glare of the morning sunlight at the frocked man standing behind Ryan. "Who's he?"

"He is Father Abaddan. And this is a wedding. Ours."

Mia's eyes went wide. "A w-wedding?"

"Yes. I'm going to have you if I have to leg shackle you to me," he smiled.

"But Ryan, I'm not dressed for a wedding," she said dazedly, stupidly.

Ryan laughed and entered her house, the priest following him in. "You look beautiful."

"I don't want to get married."

"Of course you do," Ryan countered. "You just don't realize it yet." He pulled a ring box out of his pocket and got down on one knee before her.

"Will you be my wife, Mia mine?"

Mia felt overwhelmed. She looked at the priest as if for guidance, and the old man smiled gently at her, offering no help. "I can't get married," she whispered.

"Sure you can. So long as I'm the groom."

He took her left hand and placed the diamond ring upon her finger. It was a perfect fit. "Will you marry me?" he asked again.

Mia felt her heart crack. She looked down at the ring on her finger, her hand still clasped in his. "You don't want to marry me."

"Yes I do."

"I don't know what to say."

"Say yes, silly," he laughed.

"Living with me will be dangerous," she pointed out.

"Living with any female is dangerous if you ask me. Why should you be so different? Marry me, Mia. Take the chance. I promise I'll make you very happy."

Mia felt the tears slip down her face. "I know you will."

"So say yes."

Mia felt something like joy flood through her. Could she really take the chance? She wanted to—oh how desperately she wanted to. But should she?

"Make me a happy man, Mia. Please say yes."

Mia smiled and felt her heart flood over with love. "Y-yes."

"I promise that— What did you say?"

"I said yes." She clutched his hands tight. "Yes. Yes. Yes. I'll marry you."

"Woo hoo!" He swung her up into his arms and twirled about. "I love you so much, Mia."

"I love you too, Ryan. I really do."

He embraced her then turned her so that they both faced Father Abaddan. "Let's get this wedding going. I'm ready for a wedding night."

Mia laughed, then wept with joy as they were united in holy matrimony.

The fire that always crept just below her skin seemed to dim and sputter out. How long this peace would last she didn't know. But then, no one knew what would happen in their future. It was the way things were.

So long as Ryan was with her, she could learn to live with that.

About the Author

છ

Sherri L. King lives in the American Deep South with her husband, artist and illustrator Darrell King. Critically acclaimed author of *The Horde Wars* and *Moon Lust* series, her primary interests lie in the world of action packed paranormals, though she's been known to dabble in several other genres as time permits.

Sherri welcomes comments from readers. You can find her website and email address on her author bio page at www.ellorascave.com.

Enjoy These Excerpts From:
Manaconda

Copyright © Sherri L. King, Lora Leigh and Jaid Black, 2004.

All Rights Reserved, Ellora's Cave, Inc.

Sacred Eden

Sherri L. King

"I think that, for once, I am actually looking forward to this visit to the surface world," Sid admitted to his wife.

"Well, now that the Daemons are reduced to nothing more than a handful of stragglers, I can see why. Without them to worry about, it'll be a field trip for us instead of a battle," Cady chuckled.

"This is true. But long before the Daemons began escaping into the world of humans, it was rare that I had any true interest in visiting there."

"But that was before you had me to take you to all the fun and happening places up there," Cady teased, buckling her *Sig-Sauer* 9mm P-226 pistol to her black-clad thigh. Though she didn't expect any danger tonight—it had been almost a year since the last Daemon attack after all—it never hurt to be prepared. The long skirt of her reverend-style overcoat would hide any evidence of the weapon should she garner too many curious stares…she hoped. But no way was she leaving her new favorite weapon behind.

"Baby," he chided, "I have my doubts that you even know of one such place. Before you became one of us, all your days and nights were spent working and fighting Daemons. You had no time for such idle pursuits as fun."

"Ooh, that was cold. I should spank you for that one," Cady mock-pouted, knowing that his words were true.

"Not before I spank you first," he quipped back with an exaggerated leer.

Pulling his long, black hair into a ponytail at his nape and securing it with a strip of rawhide, Sid strode over to an intricately carved wooden side-table that stood by the door. Cady couldn't help but admire the play of his roped muscles beneath the tight material of his black clothing. His tight, black, sexy clothing.

Tonight they wore no armor, as they might have but a year before when evil Daemons ran rampant over the earth. But they both preferred wearing dark colors so as to blend in with the night as they roamed above. Old habits died hard, it seemed, despite the lack of danger.

And they *had* to roam at night after all—Shikars were ultra-sensitive to the sunlight. Their race had dwelled in darkness for so long—thousands of years—that tolerance for the bright rays of daylight had been bred right out of them And though Cady had once been human herself—turned Shikar only by the powerful magic in the semen of her husband—she had not yet tested the theory that she might still be able to walk in the light.

She wasn't afraid of the risk, not really. But Obsidian had forbidden her to even think of testing the resilience of her flesh in the rays of the sun. While she wasn't always inclined to willingly heed a command that her beloved—yet arrogant— husband gave her, she had seen the stark fear in his eyes as he worried over the possibility of her injury, or even death. So she had, for once, decided to let her dearest have his way.

Giving up the sun was such a small price to pay for this new life she'd gained. A loving husband, a perfect son, the power to create fire with her mind and her will, and the ability to shoot deadly, poisonous blades from her flesh—without any real pain or effort—were huge boons that made the loss of daylight seem almost insignificant in comparison.

"I almost forgot, Desondra brought this when she came for Armand." Sid's deep, sexy voice snapped Cady out of her wandering thoughts.

She reached for the piece of folded parchment he held out for her. "Ah." She nodded when she realized what it was. "I'd meant to ask you about this earlier."

It was the main reason they were going up to the surface world, this piece of parchment. Or rather, what was written on it.

"Let's see...Edge wants some peaches, Emily wants some new handcuffs—how the heck am I going to find 'official police handcuffs'? Steffy wants some hot dogs and the new *Hooverphonic* cd, Cinder wants some clove cigarettes and," she paused, incredulous, "a DVD of *The Three Stooges*. You gotta be kidding me. No wonder the generators keep running out of fuel...Steffy and Cinder are hooking up goodness knows how many devices to 'em."

Sid only chuckled and buckled up his knee-high, oxblood boots.

"Where was I? *Hmm*...Desondra wants chocolate, Agate wants—oh lord—*fuck-me-pumps*!" Cady laughed over that last request on the list. She looked up at Sid, whose Shikar-yellow eyes were wide with avid curiosity over such a request. "She actually wrote 'fuck-me-pumps' on here. The woman never ceases to surprise me."

Knight Stalker

Lora Leigh

Okay, so she had prayed for adventure, freedom. Something that would shake her world up and make her live, for a change. A lover unlike any other. An event, an experience that would change her life. Bliss hadn't meant learning that the man she completely lusted after was a vampire. She could have lived without that knowledge. It wasn't one of those pieces of information that she felt she needed to know.

Bliss opened her apartment door slowly the next afternoon. As normal, the shades and curtains were flung wide, the early morning sunshine piercing the room in wonderful, vibrant rays. A whimper of thankfulness escaped her lips as she rushed into the living room and locked the door behind her quickly.

She couldn't believe what she had seen the night before. She couldn't make herself shake the prayer that it had all been a nightmare. She would awaken soon. All she had to do was pinch herself enough to wake up. Because, despite what she had seen, despite the fear, the overpowering need to run, she had been aroused. Aroused and drawn to the dark vision as nothing she had ever been in her life.

It had made her so damned hot she had needed to change her panties even as she ran for her life, because she had creamed them outrageously.

She tossed her keys to the table beside her and leaned her head against the panel, breathing heavily, exhausted from her fight to stay hidden the night before, certain that she was being stalked. That the monster she had glimpsed in the bar's private room was but one step behind her...

"Well, perhaps more than one step."

Shock exploded in her chest as she turned, eyes wide, and confronted the dark vision of her worst nightmares. He stood in front of the window. The bright rays of the sun surrounded his tall, muscular body, created a halo around his thick hair and held his expression in shadow.

She blinked, certain she was making him up.

"Shouldn't you be in a coffin or something?" she gasped, her eyes wide as she felt her pussy moistening further. This was too much. She wanted to fuck a monster. She must have lost her mind.

"You watch too much television." He tsked gently, his midnight-blue eyes filled with laughter and promise. "That is the trouble with the world and those who inhabit it. They rely only on the legends and the tales passed down from generation to generation or created within the pages of a fiction novel. Yes, my dear, vampires exist." His voice lowered to a dark, sensual throb. "And the rules were never truly recorded properly."

She could hear the amusement in his voice, the cool mocking knowledge that he had won. Wet pussy or not, she wasn't going to deal with this right now. Her hands gripped the doorknob as she tried to turn it, to escape, to find a way to process this new information.

Except the door wouldn't open. Her hands twisted the knob, while jerky whimpers that should have been violent screams tore from her throat.

"Bliss, chill out." He was right behind her.

Bliss swung around, her fist clenched, aiming for his head as she swung her arm. In an instant it was caught within his broad palm as he stared down at her with dark, hot eyes.

"Such violent tendencies," he murmured, his voice rough and deep as he pinned her against the door. "If I didn't know better, Bliss, I would think you didn't like me anymore."

He was laughing at her. She stared up at him in a haze of fury, fear and arousal, seeing the amusement in his gaze as he watched her. The fury and fear she understood, but the arousal made zero sense to her way of thinking.

"I would like you better with a stake in your heart," she snapped, struggling against him as he held her easily.

"Bliss, I am not going to hurt you," he said softly as he pushed her hands against the door, his body flush against hers, trapping her against the panel as he transferred her wrists to one hand. The other stroked over her neck gently.

Devilish Dot

Jaid Black

Two crimson eyes flew open. Air rushed into depleted lungs, his concaved, translucent silver chest rapidly expanding to its total musculature and size. Deadly fangs exploded from his gums. Lethal claws and talons shot out from his fingers and toes.

She is near…

He had been cocooned for one hundred earth years, his body and mind in *gorak* — the Khan-Gori term for "the sleep of the dead". *Gorak* comes every five hundred Yessat Years and occurs between each of a Barbarian's seven lives. Five hundred and one Yessat Years he had spent without *her*, without the one. He mayhap ended his first life in defeat of finding her, but his second life was about to commence —

Vaidd Zyon could feel her, could sense her, could smell her. He took a slow, deep breath, nostrils flaring and eyes briefly closing, as he inhaled her scent.

It *was* her.

His Bloodmate.

He had evolved in *gorak*. Stronger. Deadlier. More ferocious than ever he was in his first life. 'Twas time to begin his second lifetime.

Every day, every hour, every second of the five hundred and one Yessat Years he'd spent without her had been akin to the blackest abyss. No sense of hope. No sense of joy. No reason to wish to evolve in *gorak* and begin the next five hundred years without the one who had been born that she might complete him. Many a day Vaidd had felt like ending it — forever.

But his pack needed him. Verily, he was his sire's heir apparent. And so he'd carried on. Grim. Lethal. Merciless. But he'd carried on.

Vaidd took another deep breath and, once more, inhaled the scent of his Bloodmate. She was close. Very close.

The beating of his heart stilled for one angry, possessive moment when his senses confirmed something else:

She was not alone. Other males drew near.

A low growl rumbled in his throat until it turned into a deafening roar. In an explosion of violence, hunger, possession, and desire, Vaidd burst from his cocoon and shot into the air, his twelve-foot wings expanding on a predator's ruthless cry. The instinct to return to his pack was overridden by the more primal need to track his Bloodmate — and kill any male that might touch her.

Her scent was strong, intoxicating. Bewitching. She *would* be his and no other's.

She belonged to him.

* * * * *

Dot's eyelids blinked in rapid succession as she slowly, groaningly, came to. Her forehead wrinkled in incomprehension as she glanced around. "Well hell's goddamn bells," she muttered. "Where in the world am I?"

What a night! she thought tragically. Turning off the engine, she opened the door of her car and arose from the driver's seat. The rain must have ended and brought a thick fog with a cold front in its stead, for she could barely see anything at all and felt so chilled to the bone that it was as if she'd woken up in the middle of the Arctic.

Frowning, she narrowed her eyes and ran her hands up and down her goose-pimpled arms, trying to make heads or tails of her location. But the fog was thick. She couldn't see anything at all other than what was in the immediate vicinity of her car. Not even with the headlights still shining off into the distance. What she thought the oddest, however, was that the tree she had collided with was no longer anywhere to be seen. But she'd definitely struck it…

Immediately noting that the oak she'd made impact with had left a highly noticeable dent in the driver's side door, she angrily slammed the thing shut and harrumphed. Feeling in true drama-queen form, she lifted the back of her hand up to her forehead and sighed.

Great! This is just terrific! I haven't had almost-sex in four years, actual sex in eight years, I spent my Friday night driving through a horrible rainstorm in the middle of nowhere trying to find Nowhere…and now on top of everything else, my insurance premium will go through the roof!

A lesser woman wouldn't be able to pull herself together, she thought on a sniff. A lesser woman would come undone.

Dot decided she was a lesser woman.

A warbled cry of anger, frustration—no doubt partially sexual in origin!—and dismay began in her belly, gurgled up to her throat, and exploded from her mouth in a shrill, shrieking cry. She kicked the door in three times for good measure with the toe of one of the black high-heeled shoes she wore. (The ones that perfectly coordinated with her pink suit ensemble, if she did say so herself.) Might as well. The damn door would need fixed anyway!

That accomplished, she screamed again, this time longer and louder. She jumped up and down like a mad jack-in-the-box as she shrieked, fists tight and nostrils flaring. Her hair came undone out of the tight bun she'd had it coiled in, but it didn't matter. Her tantrum was making her feel better. Much better, in fact.

A low growl pierced the quiet of the night. And then another. The growls sounded as if off from a distance, but growing closer by the millisecond.

Dot immediately shut-up. She ceased jumping. Her ears perked up and her eyes widened as she looked around.

Nothing.

The fog was so thick and all-encompassing that she couldn't see anything. And the growling had just altogether stopped—practically as soon as it had begun. She swallowed a bit roughly, wondering to herself if this was what people meant by the old colloquialism, "the quiet before the storm".

Dot hastily arrived at the conclusion that she didn't want to know.

Deciding she could finish up being a lesser woman later— like in the safety of her home!—the sex toy maker determined it would, perhaps, be in her best interests to get the hell out of dodge. Like now.

What a night! What a night! What a night!

Why an electronic book?

We live in the Information Age—an exciting time in the history of human civilization, in which technology rules supreme and continues to progress in leaps and bounds every minute of every day. For a multitude of reasons, more and more avid literary fans are opting to purchase e-books instead of paper books. The question from those not yet initiated into the world of electronic reading is simply: *Why?*

1. *Price.* An electronic title at Ellora's Cave Publishing and Cerridwen Press runs anywhere from 40% to 75% less than the cover price of the exact same title in paperback format. Why? Basic mathematics and cost. It is less expensive to publish an e-book (no paper and printing, no warehousing and shipping) than it is to publish a paperback, so the savings are passed along to the consumer.

2. *Space.* Running out of room in your house for your books? That is one worry you will never have with electronic books. For a low one-time c ost, you can purchase a handheld device specifically designed for e-reading. Many e-readers have large, convenient screens for viewing. Better yet, hundreds of titles can be stored within your new library—on a single microchip. There are a variety of e-readers from different manufacturers. You can also read e-books on

your PC or laptop computer. (Please note that Ellora's Cave does not endorse any specific brands. You can check our websites at www.ellorascave.com or www.cerridwenpress.com for information we make available to new consumers.)

3. *Mobility.* Because your new e-library consists of only a microchip within a small, easily transportable e-reader, your entire cache of books can be taken with you wherever you go.

4. *Personal Viewing Preferences.* Are the words you are currently reading too small? Too large? Too... ANNOYING? Paperback books cannot be modified according to personal preferences, but e-books can.

5. *Instant Gratification.* Is it the middle of the night and all the bookstores near you are closed? Are you tired of waiting days, sometimes weeks, for bookstores to ship the novels you bought? Ellora's Cave Publishing sells instantaneous downloads twenty-four hours a day, seven days a week, every day of the year. Our webstore is never closed. Our e-book delivery system is 100% automated, meaning your order is filled as soon as you pay for it.

Those are a few of the top reasons why electronic books are replacing paperbacks for many avid readers.

As always, Ellora's Cave and Cerridwen Press welcome your questions and comments. We invite you to email us at Comments@ellorascave.com or write to us directly at Ellora's Cave Publishing Inc., 1056 Home Avenue, Akron, OH 44310-3502.

THE
☥ ELLORA'S CAVE ☥
LIBRARY

Stay up to date with Ellora's Cave Titles in
Print with our Quarterly Catalog.

TO RECIEVE A CATALOG,
SEND AN EMAIL WITH YOUR NAME
AND MAILING ADDRESS TO:

CATALOG@ELLORASCAVE.COM

OR SEND A LETTER OR POSTCARD
WITH YOUR MAILING ADDRESS TO:

CATALOG REQUEST
c/o ELLORA'S CAVE PUBLISHING, INC.
1056 HOME AVENUE
AKRON, OHIO 44310-3502

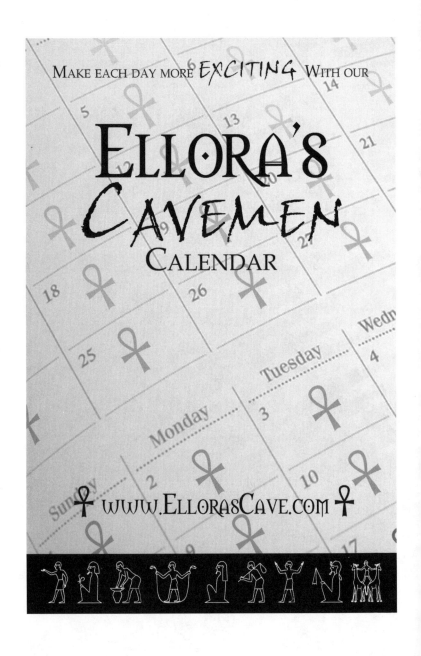

MAKE EACH DAY MORE EXCITING WITH OUR

ELLORA'S CAVEMEN

CALENDAR

WWW.ELLORASCAVE.COM

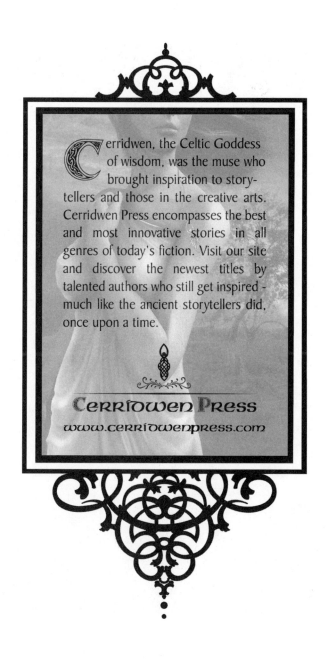

erridwen, the Celtic Goddess of wisdom, was the muse who brought inspiration to story-tellers and those in the creative arts. Cerridwen Press encompasses the best and most innovative stories in all genres of today's fiction. Visit our site and discover the newest titles by talented authors who still get inspired - much like the ancient storytellers did, once upon a time.